Emma Franieczek worked as cabin crew for two and a half years. Her first collection of short stories Living the Dream is a fictionalised telling of the world of cabin crew and was inspired by the experiences she had and the eclectic mix of people she met. She studied Creative Writing at London South Bank University and is also interested in dance, circus, cabaret and theatre. She currently lives in London.

To Kris, Mum and Dad.

Without their constant support this book wouldn't have been possible.

Contents

Living the Dream

Crew Night

I'm not gunna lie, I'm a little bit drunk, just a smudge.

"Jack. Jack!"

I'm stood at the bar of the club, not a very nice club, but the drinks are strong and the pop music's loud. I ruffle my hair to make sure it looks the right amount of *messed up bed hair* and hot! Suzi is shouting my name. Oops I'm in my fantasy world again; the one where the hot bartender wraps his arms around me and I wrap my hands around his cock. She hands me two cocktails with a big drunken grin on her face too. Two-for-one drinks all night, it'd be rude not to. Her brown bob shapes her face and her lace little black dress frames her body and her cleavage.

"Thanks Ian," we say in unison. He smiles back, well mainly at Suzi, with that smug 'I'm a pilot, I'm richer than all of you put together' look on his face. I stop smiling. He's wearing an expensive polo shirt, I think he thinks it makes him look fashionable but apparently nobody has told him he just doesn't suit polo shirts, or that chinos don't go with polo's, or brown shoes, BROWN SHOES; poor Ian. I grab Suzi and we head back to the dance floor.

"Where the fuck has she gone?" I scream into her ear as I glance around the packed room, sweaty bodies hidden by smoke machine fog.

"There!" she points and she's right. There's Kate, standing on tiptoes even in her stilettos, reaching up to meet the mouth of Pervert Pete or Player Pete depending on who you're talking to. Either way it's not good.

"Ewww," I scream as my face scrunches up in disgust. I look at Suzi and she's pulling the exact same face.

"Why?" she cries. "Why Kate, why?" This is aimed more at me than the victim herself. Even if Kate could hear over the music, she's so far gone she wouldn't notice us screaming at her.

"Do we save her?" I ask.

Before I get an answer Kaylee runs up to me and puts her arms around my neck. She pouts so I take this as an offer to pick her up and simultaneously spill my drinks all down us. With her legs straddling me I try to spin around but my feet are stuck to the floor and we almost fall over; the group of lads behind catch us. Kaylee, laughing and smiling, falls into their arms instead. I get the evils. Damn straights, but she doesn't notice and she's off again.

I turn to Suzi and laugh, she half joins in. A lot of people disapprove of Kaylee, but hey, I think she's fun.

The same place, the same music, the same people, the same time every week. If we're not working on a

Wednesday night, or Thursday morning for that matter, we're here. Me and Suzi pull out our classic dance moves to the best tunes and sing the lyrics to the songs we know and make up the lyrics to the songs we don't. It's a good job neither of us is on the pull, we wouldn't get very far.

Charlie and Ian walk over to us from the bar and I almost take Charlie out with a long flailing arm. She ducks and karate chops me right in the stomach. Ouch. We all start laughing as I apologise, well, all apart from Ian. He just stands there, nose in the air. Charlie joins the dancing and pulls Ian in. He submits and performs an awkward-dad dance for about two minutes, then hand gestures to Suzi to see if she wants a cigarette. She nods and repeats the action to me. I shake my head and carry on, in full flow, pushing others out of my way.

Charlie tugs on my arm, "Where did those two go?" I repeat the smoking gesture and she raises an eyebrow. "Is that all?"

I shrug my shoulders. I don't think Suzi is into that, or him, but it's crew night and I need another drink. I hand signal to Charlie for a drink and we head to the bar.

Charlie is one of those girls who has curves in all the right places but she always wears clothes that cover them. I don't know why because if she's drunk enough we all get a good flash.

"Shots?" I ask but Charlie doesn't answer, she's looking around the club so I order four anyway

3

from the cute as fuck bartender. That's it, you bend over and get that Sambuca from the bottom shelf; god such a good arse.

"Where's Kate?" Charlie shouts in my ear. I look around trying to spot them again and I see Kate and Pete holding hands, walk past us towards the door. I grab Kate's hand.

"Where you going?" I shout. Her eyes and smile widen as she nods towards Pete. I try and pull her away but he seems to be leaning on her tiny frame as much as she's leaning on him.

"No, no, no, no!" I shake my head but it makes me a bit dizzy. She just nods hers even more.

"Come stay at mine," I say but she's already let go of my hand. She waves her cute wave, still smiling, still nodding towards Pete in case I hadn't noticed. I look at Charlie.

"Uh oh," she mouths to me.

I let out a deep sigh and we clink our shot glasses and down them one after the other. Our faces scrunch and our heads get a hit of alcohol. As Charlie comes back into focus I shout: "Dance!" and off we go again into the crowd.

Ian and Suzi find us in the crowd. He's smiling now, with his hand on her back leading her forward. Get off her, I think. When she's close enough I smile at her then give him the evils, although I may just look drunk or sleepy instead of intimidating.

"Kate's gone," I tell Suzi.

"I thought she was coming back to yours?" she shouts in my ear and I smell the smoke on her breath, I kind of like it in a way. It reminds me of him. And that reminds me to check my phone.

"No, she's gone back with Pete!" We exchange scrunched faces again.

"Ewwww!" She echoes me. I reply with a nod and a knowing smile that says: I know right!

One new message, my phone tells me. I get a tingle in my stomach; I love the beginnings of relationships.

Hope ur having a gdnite without me ☹ *Have fun wit the girls! Can't wait to see u. Goin bed now. Nitenite, I love u xxxxx*

Aghhh my stomach tingles even more, but I've no signal to reply. He's asleep anyway, I'll make sure he gets something cute to wake up to.

Charlie is trying to look at my phone to see who I'm texting. Can't let her see.

"Kaylee's back!" I shout in her face. She smiles at me, still looking glamorous and less drunk than me; that's not on. She's brought with her Will and Ant, joy! Probably the only two straight male cabin crew in the whole world. They stare at any girl who walks past, dancing behind them, and when they're not, they compete for Kaylee's attention. She gives it to them, dancing, grinding actually. You can actually smell sex in this place.

Kaylee turns her attention towards Suzi, she takes her by the hand and spins her around. Standing behind Suzi she grabs her hips and they sway together. Ian, Will and Ant stop and stare, mouths open and everything. The girls keep dancing as if no one is watching, even though other people have stopped and are staring as well. Oh really. Charlie clicks her fingers in front of their faces and the guys literally snap out of it and close their mouths. Suzi and Kaylee split apart. It's as if they were dancing for the attention or something.

"How's Josh?" Will asks me. Ahhh the obligatory boyfriend question.

"Fine. He's on earlies." I reply.

And that's it, end of conversation. I keep dancing and singing with Suzi and Charlie, trying to ignore the boys' dribbling. People ask me about Josh more often than they ask me how I am. I am here too you know. I am an individual not half of a whole that encompasses Josh. I've mentioned this to Josh, how at work we are the same person to a lot of people but it doesn't bother him. Fuck. Don't think about them. Don't think about Josh. He doesn't come out anymore now anyways. He'd rather be tucked up on the sofa, watching shit on TV with hot chocolate. He's only twenty-six for god sake. I said don't think about Josh!

Even Ian's had enough of the straights, he's off home. He kisses all the girls on the cheek, shakes Ant and then Will by the hand, strong, firm, and then turns to me. Do I get a kiss or a hand shake? Hand shake, it seems, limp, as if I can't handle it. I'll tell you something, buddy, I can take it! Yeah. He's a man of few words and it's too loud anyway so we wave bye and he's off. What time is it anyway, it's only early. Well actually it's almost 2am but still…

Charlie's on her phone, still bobbing, still texting. Suzi has closed her eyes, her hair falling in front of her face and is dancing in her own world. Ant has found some girl from another airline to grind on him instead. Will and Kaylee are busy giggling and play fighting. Come on guys! Dance with me.

"Dance with me!"

Charlie looks up from her phone and smiles. "In a minute."

So I stop and stare at her and wait one minute. She looks up at me again and laughs. "Ok."

Somehow we're in a dance off. I'm clapping on the outside of the circle as Suzi pulls me in. I know this one. We even count in five, six, seven, eight, and our routine begins. Luckily it's not that hard so there's only a small chance of falling arse over tit. No matter

7

how many drinks we have, we've got this one. We're in unison, this is awesome. Pretty sure I should have been a dancer.

Now Kaylee's in the circle and we're out. Oh. Oh I see. She doesn't need a partner, or a dance routine. She looks hot, damn her, she looks good. Someone else I don't know jumps in and Will pulls Kaylee out of the circle.

I'm shouting, "Fight, fight, fight!" No? Ok then.

She's ok, not as good as Kaylee, not as good as us. I need some men in the circle, need me some eye candy. I 'accidentally' trip and nudge a guy to the circle. Hello biceps. I'm stroking his arms. Stop it.

"Sorry," I say and die a little inside.

But it does the trick. Everyone is cheering and yep he's dancing. Yum. Get off him! Get off him! Stupid girl, he doesn't want to dance with you.

"Get off him!" Oh I said that out loud, people are looking.

"Wait where did Charlie go? I can walk. You don't need to hold me up!" I'm still shouting. It's loud outside, or my ears are quiet, I don't know.

"She went home like half an hour ago," Suzi says.

"She didn't say goodbye to me."

"She didn't say goodbye to me either! I just saw her leaving."

I stop walking, wasn't getting anywhere fast anyway.

"I'm calling her. I'm doing it." I get out my phone, oh, oh dear. "I can't see the numbers."

"I'll do it, give it here." She takes my phone.

"Careful, don't drop it. Why aren't you drunk?"

"I am, just not as drunk as you." She bops my nose.

"NO," I scream. People turn to stare at me. "What you looking at. She got my nose."

"Shhh. Sorry. Do you want to call Charlie?"

"Yes!"

"Ok, calling." She hands me the phone.

"She's not answering. Answer. Charlie. Voicemail?"

Suzi's laughing at me.

"Charlie, where are you? Where did you go? Well you went home, I know, but where are you? You didn't even say goodbye, that's not very nice now is it? No, it's not very nice. Suzi's laughing at me, stop laughing."

"You're funny, I can't help it." Still laughing. "Leave her alone now."

"She says I'm funny. She says I have to leave you alone now. So BYE! See I said goodbye to you. I'm not happy with you. Ok night night, sleep tight. Love you."

"Here's your phone." I give it to her.

"It's your phone, Jack."

"Oh yeah." Now I'm laughing. I am funny. "Come on. Jump on." I bend over and almost fall.

"What? Piggy back?"

"Yeah, come on, piggy back to the taxi rank."

"Yeah! When we get back to yours can we keep drinking?"

"Of course, who do you think I am? Wait, Ouch!" Why am I on the floor? Why is Suzi on the floor? I look behind me. Why are my shoes so far away? She's laughing again but holding her head.

"Ouch. You dropped me!"

We're both laughing; holding our heads because they hit the ground. My knees hurt.

"My shoes!" We laugh more and more. I can't get my shoes on. They're so far away! "Oh no, my phone. It's ok, it's ok, don't panic."

"Shit, my handbag!"

She gets her handbag, I get my shoes. I have to call him. No he's asleep. I have to text him. OK.

"I have to text him."

"Who? Oh." We smile. I like smiling.

Hey babe. Hope ur sleping gd. Im bit drank. I lobe u. Wish u were here xxxxxxxxxxxxx

I think I'm saying this out loud. I hope not.

"Is it bad that I'm saying I love you, and it's not to my boyfriend?"

"Yep, Kinda." We laugh.

"But I do though, I actually think I love him."

"I know sweetie, I know." She smiles and strokes my hair. "But what about Josh?"

"I know. Josh." I feel sad. "Oh, Taxi!" I wave at it. I run at it. I hope I make it without falling over.

LGW

"Answer the phone, please answer the phone." Ben begs under his breath.

Jack answers a mumble into the phone.

"It's me, Ben, can you let me in?"

"Let you in where?" Jack says confused and sleepy.

"Your house, I'm outside." It is two in the afternoon but Ben's not surprised that Jack is still in bed after crew night. He knows only too well the effect of the mix of drinks, the *God-knows when* bed time, and tired feet.

"Oh, yeah, ok," Jack replies.

Don't go back to sleep, please don't go back to sleep, Ben begs, again to himself. He waits outside on the doorstep, rocking from foot to foot. Jack's terraced town house is near the centre of town; his mum and dad help him with the rent payments. Ben still lives at home away from the crew who spill out of almost every door in this neighbourhood: different airlines, different crews, same life style. He looks around to make sure no one else is watching. If this were a western a tumble weed would roll by. An upturned shopping cart at the end of the road lies dormant; empty bottles worshipping it. Someone had fun last night, Ben thinks to himself as he watches it, immobile. No cars, no movement. The cabin crew who live in this road are either sleeping or working. At last Jack opens the door.

"Hey!" Jack says and leans in to kiss Ben, but instead of reciprocating Ben pushes him inside the house; instantly feeling bad.

"Sorry, Sorry, I just, I don't, I can't…" Ben tries to talk but doesn't know what to say. Jack closes the door behind Ben, a little upset, confused, and sleepy. He wasn't expecting a 'booty call' last night and even less so now. He sees Ben's face, shaped by his neat hair and neat blue uniform, contorted.

"What's wrong, Ben you look awful; not ugly just, like you're really angry or really scared or something." He pulls Ben into his arms and hugs him close. Even though Jack is only wearing shorts and a thin t-shirt Ben feels the warmth from Jack's body flood into his; smothering him with homeliness. Ben hadn't realised he himself was shivering, not from the cold but the shock. He looks up into Jack's concerned and confused green eyes. Pushing his face into Jack's neck, he longs for the warmth, the comfort. Jack rests his head on Ben's.

"What's wrong?" Jack asks again rubbing Ben's back, cocooning him with his embrace.

Jack is now used to Ben's insecurities from the past couple of months, knowing that a hug can go a long way in Ben's book. Before Ben there was Aldo, much more confident, Italian, a dancer. He left the airline almost as soon as he started; a lucky escape for Jack. For the few weeks they were seeing each other, Aldo had almost let it slip three times. When he left Jack breathed a sigh of relief. So did Josh. Ben is much quieter, sweeter, and Jack knows how to make him happy; he loves the feeling of being needed, wanted so badly. He kisses Ben's cheek.

"I... I..." Ben pulls away from him slightly to look into his face again then instantly looks away. "It's stupid."

"No it's not, tell me."

"It is, it's stupid, I shouldn't have come."

"Look I can see it's upsetting you so whatever it is, just tell me," Jack demands with a yawn.

"I've been outed."

"What?" Jack is still rubbing his eyes free of last night.

"At work, Kath, she kept asking me all these question." When he thinks about Kath he goes back to being angry. He tries to conceal this from Jack, which leaves him feeling scared instead, hoping Jack won't be angry at what he has to say, what he has just said. "Like am I seeing anyone, who, where, when."

"How dare she, it's none of her business." Ben sees the anger flare up in Jack's eyes but is it directed at him or Kath? He can't tell.

"I didn't want to say much, but she wouldn't shut up." Don't cry, she's not worth it, Ben tells himself, feeling the tears waiting to explode on Jack's shoulder. Don't cry.

"Don't cry, it's ok. What did you say to her: fuck off Kath?" This shocks Ben into laughing. Finally he starts to feel a bit better. This is why he came; Jack has the ability to shock anyone into laughter with his foul mouth, but Ben's stomach still aches with sickness.

"I wish. I just said I'm seeing someone out of work, no one knows him and I don't really want to talk about it." Ben, is scared for Jack, scared for both of them but most of all, selfishly, for himself. He feels the shiver spread up his spine, but what is the fear about?

"Ok that's fine then isn't it?" Jack wipes away the tears that have not listened to Ben's pleas and are running down his face.

"Well…"

"Come upstairs and have a cup of tea, yeah? Suzi's still in bed, bless her."

Ben thinks of jumping on her to wake her up, pretending that everything's fine, but it takes all his energy just to walk up the stairs. He feels totally deflated.

"Suzi!" Jack shouts up the second set of stairs. "Ben's here!"

A mumble comes from the next level up and moments later they can hear her banging around, as she tries to get up.

Jack sits Ben at the small table in his small kitchen. There are pizza boxes lying on the side from last night and half-drunk drinks. But apart from that his place is quite clean, as usual. He puts the kettle on and sits down next to Ben.

"Josh isn't coming over is he?" The boyfriend. Always be careful of the boyfriend. Ben hates it, but he doesn't hate Josh. Sometimes he thinks he should, or that Josh should hate him, but Josh has no idea, Ben reassures himself. He's pretty sure Josh has no idea.

"No, no, don't worry about that. I'm not seeing him till later. I'm glad you came to see me." Jack smiles and this time Ben lets Jack kiss his lips. Suzi comes in the kitchen, gets a glass out and fills it with cold water.

"I feel like shit. I blame you, Jack."

She doesn't look great either. Her make-up is smudged all down her face and her hair is poking out in strange directions. Her outfit matches Jack's: shorts and a t-shirt of his. "Pizza was a good idea, though." With that, she opens one of the pizza boxes and takes out a cold slice. Jack laughs and Ben attempts a smile.

"Sorry, Ben." She walks over and kisses him on the cheek, then resumes her position, leaning on the counter, like she can't hold herself up properly. "How are you?"

Jack answers for him. "Kath's being an arsehole at work."

"When is she not?" Suzi replies with a mouthful of pizza. "What happened?"

"She kept asking me if I was seeing anyone, who it was, that kind of stuff. Then when I wouldn't tell her anymore she went and told everyone else in the crew room." Ben explains again.

"Remind me how she got the job as manager again?" Suzi remarks.

Jack turns to Ben. "Have you told anyone you're gay?"

"Not really."

"So she just starts spreading rumours about you, right in front of your face." Jack is getting angry again now.

"Basically, yes," Ben says, quietly, feeling stupid again.

"Fuck sake! She can't just talk shit about your personal life to anyone. She's your fucking manager," Suzi bursts in.

"Suzi's right, she can't do that."

Don't cry, not again Ben keeps telling himself but his body refuses to listen. He takes a deep breath.

"But she has." Not knowing what else to say Ben tries to explain his jumbled thoughts. "I just wanted to be able to tell people myself, I know most people already think I am but they haven't bothered with all the questions."

"But now they will. That's what you're thinking?" Jack finishes his sentence for him.

"Yeah."

Ben thinks of Aldo. Someone he never met but knows all about though gossip; a dancer, a drama queen. Ben can't imagine what Jack ever saw in him, he's completely the opposite of himself. Is that what they, everyone, expects? Ben wonders, for me to become camp, talk in a higher voice, wear tight clothes and buff up my body? Just because I'm gay? That's not what he wants, but is it what other people expect? Ben's mind is confused with so many questions, most of all, why do people care? Why should they? Yes I'm cabin crew, and surprise surprise, I'm gay! But that does not make me a queen. I am, just, me. Ben reminds himself, trying to be strong. It's a shame he can't say these words out loud, or believe them.

There's silence for the first time. Suzi breaks it.

"Don't be angry at yourself. You're allowed to be angry but at her, not yourself. She's being an absolute idiot."

"I know," Ben replies.

"She has no right to talk to people like that, or talk about you like that," Jack adds.

"I know." His reply turns to a mumble. Jack's face turns from anger to the hurt that he sees in Ben's eyes, and hugs him.

Ben wonders if even Jack and Suzi will change how they think of him now, and they already know. They've already started to change his hair, his clothes, making him more fashionable. Ben tells himself that they are taking him under their wing. I'm not gay enough to be gay, he thinks.

"It's ok. So people know now. If they ask if you're gay all you say is 'yes, and?' and they'll shut up," Jack says into Ben's shoulder.

"I just, I'm pissed off," Ben finally lets out his thoughts hugging Jack back.

"Good, you should be," says Suzi. "I mean not good that it's happened but good, get it out, you know what I mean? I think I'm still drunk."

They all laugh. The tension that had been building through the tears is released.

"The thing is, I don't want to get you in trouble," Ben says to Jack, not quite meeting his eyes.

Ben can feel Jack tense up in his arms, just a little. "Did you say my name?"

"No! Of course not."

"Then we're fine."

Ben nods, not really sure what else to do.

"Look at it this way, it's saved you a few awkward conversations at work, and will stop people trying to set you up. Apart from Kath being a arsehole, think of the positives," Jack tries a different angle.

"Ok," Ben replies but he knows he would have preferred those awkward conversations, when he was ready to talk, in his own time.

"So we're all ok? Can I go back to bed and die now?" Suzi asks.

"Of course you can go back to bed; I didn't mean to wake you. I'm sorry."

"Not at all gorgeous," She smiles. "As long as you're ok."

She turns to leave the kitchen and head back to bed, Ben tries to stop himself from saying it but without even meaning to, he blurts it out.

"Do you think I should tell me parents?"

Suzi stops. Jack and Suzi both look at each other and then at Ben. They seem to have a secret code that he can never fathom. They can understand each other's thoughts, just through an exchange of looks. "Yes? No?" They look at each other again and back to Ben.

"Honey, we can't make that decision for you," Jack says. "Do it if you're ready and you want to, but don't do it just because you feel you have to." Ben notices Jack's expression, concerned, more serious than before.

"You're only nineteen, you have plenty of time," Suzi adds.

"I think I want to," Ben replies. And he thinks, he hopes, it's true.

An hour later, Suzi, now sober, washes, dresses and offers to drive Ben over to his parents' house. They say goodbye to Jack as he's doing his hair, getting ready to see Josh. Ben watches Jack feeling jealous then, which he doesn't usually let himself do. Jack does get dressed up to see him too but this time it's different. This time Ben feels like he needs Jack with him.

As they reach Ben's street he asks Suzi, "Can we just wait here a minute?"

"Of course," she replies and they sit and wait, only a few houses away, in silence.

Ben sees number 38, Amelia's house. His ex-girlfriend Amelia's house. They were together for three years, throughout school and college. Best friends who became more, it just seemed like the next step to take, to become boyfriend and girlfriend. And Ben was happy. He found men attractive, good looking, but lots of his male friends had 'guy crushes'. His best friend said the one celebrity he'd like to sleep with the most would be David Beckham, and he was straight. Ben felt like his emotions were normal, even though he preferred looking at men's clothing on those gorgeous male models to the female ones. Amelia wanted to take it further, she was ready, she told him. He hadn't minded waiting until they were both eighteen, he was happy. Until finally she asked him; she was the first person to 'out' him, though she kept it to herself. She wasn't angry at the time. Ben was. He was angry at himself. How come he hadn't known? Maybe he was bi-sexual. Maybe it was just a phase? No. He knew that wasn't true. It was Amelia who made him accept himself.

That was only a year ago and Ben wonders why he didn't go round to hers and tell her about the business with Kath. Because she wouldn't understand, not working in aviation. Because her new boyfriend might be there. Or maybe because he doesn't want to admit that she was right all along.

Ben takes a deep breath to try and prepare himself. He takes another deep breath, then another and another, looking around at the neat detached houses, where the hedges are perfectly trimmed, the flower beds beautiful even in winter and Mrs Jackson down the road is the talk of the village with her new pond out front. Ben thinks, I can't wait to get out of here. This place, where he has lived, since childhood, now feels like a cage, trapping him here. Town is so close but it feels a million miles away from this street. Jack feels a million miles away. Breathe he reminds himself.

"It's ok." Suzi turns to Ben and says, the engine on her Peugeot still running. "You don't have to do this now if you don't want to."

"I want to, I'm just… I'm so glad you're here, with me."

She smiles and leans over the hand brake to hug him. "Of course gorgeous. I'll always be here."

He doesn't belong here. Amongst these perfect gardens; the imperfect son. He knows his parents will think it's the job, his new friends, his new hair. 'It didn't even take you a year in that job to start pretending you're something else,' they'll say. If only they knew the truth. Ben's eyes glaze over, shielding him from the perfect view. That's why I'm here I guess, he tells himself. He sighs.

"Ok, let's go."

They pull into the drive of Ben's parents' house and see his mum's car sitting waiting but not his dad's. He's not home yet, oh shit, Ben panics. Suzi turns off the engine and gets out of the car so Ben follows. She waits for him to lead the way and as they approach the door it swings open revealing Ben's beaming mother; his stomach flips.

"Hello, how was work?" she asks.

"It was fine, uneventful." He tries to sound as upbeat as she does.

"That's what I like to hear!" Ben sees her watching Suzi as they walk in through the door and remove their shoes. Sandra, Ben's mum tries to pat his hair down into what she says is a more conventional style. She hasn't given the new hair a name yet, she will.

"You can just leave them here," Ben tells Suzi as she holds her shoes politely. "Mum this is Suzi."

"Lovely to meet you. I've heard all about you, all good don't worry." Suzi blushes and laughs at Sandra's attempt at a joke.

"Do you want tea?"

"That'd be lovely, milk, one sugar please."

They move towards the immaculately clean kitchen; no leftovers of a night partying in here.

Sandra smiles and puts the kettle on, proud of her home and family, showing it off to her guests. Ben and Suzi sit down at the kitchen table as she gets the mugs and tea bags out of the cupboards.

"When will Dad be home?"

"He's just picking up your sister, should be back any minute."

Lazy cow Ben thinks to himself. Fourteen years old and she still gets Dad to pick her up from school. But that's what you get for being the baby. He doesn't want to say anything without his Dad here; not being able to bear the thought of saying it twice. "How was work?" he asks, trying to keep a conversation going.

"Oh same old, same old," Sandra replies absentmindedly whilst pouring the water and milk in the teas. "The new girl cried, Mandy shouted, well the new girl cried because Mandy shouted. Aaron broke the printer. I got to shout at some people down the phone. You know." She sugars the teas stirring. She places the mugs down in front of Ben and Suzi and joins them at the table.

Keys rattle in the door and a "Hello" is shouted through the hall from Ben's dad. Abby, his sister, walks past the kitchen to the living room not paying attention to who's in it and mutters a "Hi."

Ben realises he's holding his breath and lets out a gasp for air, for life. Ben's dad looks at him sideways and carries on. He wants to call Abby back so she can be a buffer between his parents and himself but would that work? Does she already know? Ben thinks she does but realises he doesn't want her indifference to everything; it would only follow through to him.

"Have I just missed a brew?" Ben's dad asks entering the kitchen. "Hi I'm Adam." He offers his hand out to Suzi not missing a beat.

"Suzi." She shakes his hand and smiles such a warm smile, a cabin crew smile.

Ben can feel his stomach starting to hurt from knowing what he's about to say. Looking at Suzi he tries to copy the smile but it turns into a grimace of pain.

"Ah, the lovely Suzi, nice to finally meet you," Adam says as he pours himself a tea.

Suzi looks at Ben with that same smile but questioning eyes. He smiles back and tries to reassure her that they only know the good stuff, honest. Suzi seems to understand and takes his hand for comfort. She nods and asks Adam, "Will you join us?"

"Of course. How are you Suzi, Ben?"

But Ben blurts out, "Can we talk, I need to talk." Without meaning to, the words jump from his lips and into the air, where they hang at the surprise of Ben's voice. Sandra's smile drops and she looks straight at Suzi.

"Are you pregnant?" she asks, more ordering a response than just asking.

"No, no!" Suzi laughs nervously as she looks down at their clasped hands; his squeezing hers tightly. "Oh god no."

Sandra seems to relax at this but looks confused.

"It's me Mum, I need to say something."

"Are you ok? What's wrong?" She looks at Ben now. With only a quick glance back at Suzi, she focuses on what he's saying.

"I'm fine. Please just let me say something."

"Ok," Adam says. "Talk."

He takes one last deep breath. "I don't really know how to say this so I guess I just have to put it out there." Silence, they wait, watching. Ben can't quite meet their gaze. "I'm gay."

Nothing. Nothing but silence. They look at Ben, then each other. They look at Suzi to see if this is a joke but as she looks back at them and then at Ben, they know it's not. They say nothing. Say something please, Ben pleads in his head, the silence killing him.

"Are you, are you sure?" Adam asks.

Knowing that was coming Ben replies, "I'm positive," and they fall silent again. They look away from Ben and, as if imitating him and Suzi, they hold hands. Unable to cope Ben begs, "Will you say something, please." But they don't.

Ben didn't expect to be welcomed with smiles and hugs, the way Jack greeted him. They're not a tactile family; they love each other from a distance. But he assumed they loved him and always would. That's what his mum said to him when he and Amelia broke up, one of the only friendly, rather than mothering moments of his adulthood. The silence is the biggest shock; Sandra always has something to say but not now. The friendly smile has been wiped from Adam's face and the love, the instinctive love in their eyes has faded, almost disappeared. Ben thinks he can see it turning into something else, something scary: contempt.

It's Suzi who speaks at last. "I think you have such a wonderful son. Ben is a wonderful man. He's loving and kind." But she stops speaking as his parents begin to stare at her. Their eyes are asking who she is, why she has come here and made their son tell them these lies.

"Ben, come with me," Suzi says abruptly and stands up. Ben stands as well, still holding her hand. "Like I said, you have a wonderful son. He'll be staying with me for a while, but when you realise how amazing he is, he'll come home."

He hears the words come out of Suzi's mouth but doesn't believe them. Needing to let them sink in, digest, he looks at his parents who are still sitting, their teas steaming slowly, untouched, looking up at them, then from one to the other. Ben looks away, incapable of looking at their faces any more. He lets go of Suzi's hand and they walk around Sandra and Adam, out the kitchen door, out through the hall, out the front door and back towards the car. Don't look back Ben tells himself. Don't you dare look back. Forcing himself to put one foot in front of the other he makes it to the car.

Suzi starts the car. Ben can see she's angry. He tries to feel the same but doesn't. Not knowing what he feels he thinks, I should be crying, why aren't I crying? But he doesn't actually feel anything. Suzi drives away from the house, away from his parents, his perfect family in their perfect home, but she doesn't say anything.

Ben, still in his uniform suddenly realises he doesn't have anything with him, not even a change of clothes. At last he looks back, but they are too far away now even if he could face going back inside.

As if she's read Ben's mind Suzi says "We're going shopping." So they do.

AGP

"Ready for passengers Charlie?" Jerry, my senior, asks over the PA. I poke my head out of the back galley and give a thumbs up.

"Thanks gorgeous gal. They're on their way," he says.

Joy. I'm not sure I am ready for this but here we go. Tea with lots of sugar is needed, and my second round of paracetamol today. Crew night last night was not a good idea. God only knows what time we got to bed, let alone sleep. I take out a pack of crew biscuits, stealing the bourbons before anyone else can. The rumble of noise as people talk, shout, and push their way on to the plane becomes louder as I dunk my bourbon in my tea, the quiet time is over.

I look down the cabin and see the Malaga bound passengers dumping what seems to be their entire worldly belongings into the overhead bins wherever they feel like it. Taylor's trying to help but she can barely reach the overhead bins.

Taylor, fifty years old, with the excitable nature of a toddler and about the same height too, lost her job in the recession and thought flying would be a fun new start for some reason. Well she's got the enthusiasm that's for sure; I don't know how she passed the height test though, I really don't. She doesn't give a single fuck if people are in her way and starts to climb on seats, moving people's stuff before they've even let go of it.

I finish my bourbons, self-love always comes first, sigh and pick up the PA.

"Ladies and Gentlemen, boys and girls, welcome aboard your flight to Malaga. Can we please ask you to take your seat as soon as possible to allow other passengers to board the plane. There are two areas to store your cabin baggage, in the overhead bins and underneath the seat in front of you. Please place HEAVIER items underneath the seat in front of you and smaller LIGHTER items in the overhead bins. Please leave room for other passengers to use this space as well."

Or instead I guess you could continue to ignore me and place your bags wherever the fuck you like, and just get in everyone's way. Later when you ask why we're delayed I'll inform you that it's your fault for taking your sweet fucking time. In the event of an emergency I'm sure what you really want is all your duty free alcohol in the overhead bins to fall out and crack your skull open. You partner's coat will then fall on you and scare the shit out of you as your children's loose toys roll down the cabin, tripping everyone up and meaning you can't exit the plane without joining the bundle.

"All electronic equipment must be turned off when the aircraft doors are closed. Mobile phones and other devices equipped with flight safe mode must have this turned on before the device is switched off."

I don't actually care if your phone is on or not, mine will be, but if yours is do not let me see it or I will come down on you so hard you will want to cry.

I can and I will confiscate your phone, and look through your messages and photographs. So do as you're told. I don't want to keep repeating myself, this is for your safety and because of your stupidity not mine.

After all the passengers are in their seats; the headcount is completed (first attempt); the doors are armed and crosschecked; the safety demo is done, without any mishaps (I didn't break any demo equipment, or smack anyone in the head); and the cabin secure is complete (yes sir you do have to turn off your iPod, excuse me miss can you sit up straight with your chair and armrest in the correct position? This *is* the fourth time I've asked.)

We tidy away magazines and mess in the galley, everything must be secure, apply a quick spritz of perfume and a slick of lipstick, and take our crew seats. We wait for the cabin secure call from Jerry and from my swivel seat, facing up the cabin, I can see at least three mobile phones appear, a bag is pulled out from under a seat and a couple on either side of the aisle are holding hands. I give up. Two chimes sound as my senior calls me on the PA phone.

"Cabin secure for take-off?" he asks.

"Cabin secure," I reply.

"Did you see this lot? Jaysus, one hundred and seventy four plus four babies, for feck sake; thankfully they're down your end."

"Yeah cheers," I snort.

"And one carry-off, shower o' bastards. Get the self-tan out on the duty free display and make sure they have enough alcohol, just not too much," he attempts a whisper but I'm sure the front row could probably hear him, that's if they were paying attention to anything other than themselves.

"Will do," I laugh.

"We'll work hard this sector and make our money up then next sector they'll all be ready for bed anyways; we'll turn the lights down and heating up. Send them off into a nice sleep for two and a half hours so we will. Oh yeah, flight time two and a half hours, no surprises there."

"Ok, sounds like a plan."

"Right you are, just remember, tits and teeth gorgeous. See you up there."

I turn to Taylor who's filing her nails and tell her the flight time along with how many passengers, babies and wheelchairs we have.

"Oh for fuck sake," she says.

"I'm just hoping they are ready for the lift-off ASAP. Wanna be home nice and early," I say, then regret it.

"Oh, any plans for tonight then?" And that's why I regret it. I don't want to tell her that Ian's on the Munich, which lands just before us, and I don't want to keep him waiting around to pick me up.

"Just want to get home and in bed," I say with a smile, "crew night took it out of me." I turn my head away from her. I don't need the Spanish inquisition, not now, not from her. I like my private life just that, private.

The plane jolts as it moves along over the bumps in the taxi way. I feel it lurch round to the right and know that we're queuing up for the runway; we've hit the rush hour.

Taylor starts telling me she hasn't got time to go back to bed, what with watching her dog, looking after her daughter who's due any day now and going on a date herself. She just wishes she had time for a simple cup of tea. Her voice hurts my head; she speaks likes she moves, as if she's on fast forward. I wish she would just stop for a cup of tea and take a deep breath.

The plane slowly rolls forward again, rounding off the corner and we finally reach the runway. We adopt our take-off positions, hands facing upwards underneath our thighs, heels together slightly behind our knees, elbows in and heads, well our buns really, resting lightly on the head rest. I take a quick look down the cabin and close my eyes. I feel the reassuring pull of the plane as it starts to gain speed and we rumble down the runway. My stomach sinks as we lift upwards and as my stomach re-joins the rest of my body I think of him. I think of last night.

Yes, I went out and yes I drank my fair share of alcohol. Yes, there was dancing, and laughing and flirting, no matter what your sexual orientation. Yes, Ian left fairly promptly and I followed him twenty minutes later back to his house; we got separate taxis, and when I arrived he was waiting for me. Yes, there was sex, he pulled me inside the house unable to wait, our clothes scattered the floor and stairs up to his bedroom but that wasn't my favourite part of the night. Don't get me wrong it was great but what I wanted was what came afterwards.

I'm not usually a clingy girl, I'm usually the one who falls straight asleep after sex. But with Ian, how do I describe it? The secret makes it hard for us to show our feelings for each other in public yet alone we laugh, we talk and yes we have a lot of sex. We are not together, our relationship just is, and whatever it is, for now it works. I don't allow myself the fantasy of it being long-term. But then, just as I am drifting off, I feel his arms around me; our naked bodies touching, not in a sexual way, but showing love. Those words I could never say to him, his body says to mine. With one arm underneath me and the other around me he kisses my neck goodnight. As I roll to get comfortable and turn to cuddle into his arms he kisses my forehead. I don't know whether he's asleep or awake but he never lets me go. He softly strokes me, placing small kisses on my skin as we drift in and out of sleep. If I felt vulnerable before, the embrace lets me let it go and believe in him, in us. I know in the morning he will wake up and make me breakfast, maybe give me a kiss goodbye; our relationship will become more formal in the daylight. But in the dark, in the dark I love him, and he makes it seem, whether subconsciously or not, that some part of him may love me too.

A bump awakes me and I realise I had fallen asleep on my crew seat. How is it that the most uncomfortable seat on the aircraft is the easiest to fall asleep in? I guess it's the harness that straps not just your waist in but your shoulders too. It allows the rolls and bumps of the plane to take you with it and rock you to sleep like a baby.

I look over to Taylor and she's up and pulling the carts out already. Calm down woman, we're still at a forty degree angle. I rub my eyes and then remember I am wearing make-up. Fuck. I'm hoping no passengers looked around and saw me sleeping, head lolling around and everything. Ah well. I take a another deep breath and prepare for the flight.

The chimes sound again. I pick up the PA phone. From the front, I see Jerry leaning round the bulk head and looking down the aisle at me.

"Tell her to sit the feck down for five minutes will ya, the passengers will see her and start wandering themselves. Also me and Graham are having a quick chat, so we are."

"Taylor," I call over my shoulder, "Sit down for a bit." She realises I'm on the phone and sits down, if I'd have said it on my own she'd been out in the cabin within thirty seconds, 'I'll make a start, you relax' she would've added.

Jerry gives me the thumbs up and as he hangs up I can hear his "bye,bye,bye,bye,bye,bye,bye" getting slowly further away. I close my eyes again, resting my head on my seat. His kisses flash into my mind and I quickly open my eyes to stop the thoughts.

When Jerry says it's ok to get up, more likely when he and Graham have finished talking about whatever it was, we start the service.

Can I get you anything? Would you like to purchase any drinks or snacks? Tea, coffee, sandwiches, snacks? Yes Sir, you do have to pay, yes water is £2.50. Americans are always the worst at this. Excuse me, Madam, you do not need to smack my arse to ask for another sugar sachet. No, I'm not joking that we've run out of chicken wraps, it may confuse you but it's not actually my style to play jokes on you by hiding food. We did give you prior warning that this service was taking place. We also informed you that you could find the menu in your seat pocket so please don't ask me to stand there naming everything we sell. No, I will not take your baby's dirty nappy while I'm serving food, and why the fuck are you changing your baby in the seat, we have changing facilities in the toilets, and yes we did say this over the PA, and yes there are signs on the toilets as well. With a sigh I think, god I really am living the dream, as they say.

We move onto the rubbish clear in, where things are practically thrown in your general direction, always fun. And then to the duty free shopping; jewellery, watches, perfume, aftershave, make-up, gifts, and travel essentials. Loads of shit that you don't really need, but it's cheaper than the shops so why the bloody hell not, you're on holiday. Here's a little secret, the crew fall for it too, I have the cleanser, toner, moisturiser set, the mascara, the bronzer, three perfumes, a watch, the diamanté earrings and matching bracelet, and the head phones. I don't use half of it, but, hey, I get commission on the sales.

An hour and a half later I get to sit down and have some food for myself. Graham, goes out and does another rubbish clear in and Jerry pulls the curtain across the back galley.

"Oh Jaysus, that's better, get some food down ya," he says, "what do you fancy? Chicken? Beef that tastes like chicken? Or fish, that tastes like chicken?"

"Beef please," Taylor says, as she takes it, "If that's alright with everyone," she adds taking the lid off and stirring it.

Graham comes back to the galley and we all squeeze in, eating off our laps. A passenger pops their head round the curtain and hands us their rubbish, because our hands aren't busy and neither are we, obviously. We're here to serve.

Taylor shovels her food down and re-applies her lipstick. "I'll check on the passengers in a minute just let me go toilet," she tells us and it's ok with me and Jerry if she wants to keep running around. As soon as she exits the curtained off galley we hear a shriek come from just behind it and Taylor scrambling to get back in the galley. She clings to the curtain keeping it shut. "Should've locked the door. He was just sitting there, happily reading the paper and having a shit! This isn't his house, this is where I work." She shivers at the thought and we all burst into tears of laughter.

Just as we've calmed down, we hear the toilet flush and through the gap in the curtain we see a man exit folding his newspaper. Not one of us can contain the laughter that erupts behind the curtain as he hurries back down the cabin to his seat.

I manage to finish my food through giggles and Jerry takes my rubbish from me.

"Come here to me, did you go to crew night last night?" he asks.

"Yeah," I reply, wondering where he's going with this.

"Give us the goss then." I can see Taylor's ears prick up and the internal struggle within her wanting to do everything at once: check on the passengers, clear in their rubbish, get them anything they want and yet also hear the gossip.

"Oh, tuning into galley FM as we speak," Graham adds, making himself comfortable, or as comfortable as possible on a metal box in the middle of the galley. He and Jerry giggle to each other like school girls. I think the shock on Taylor's face with the toilet incident has set them off for the rest of the flight now.

Taylor almost runs up the cabin grabbing rubbish left, right and centre and makes her way back before I've even started.

"So come on, tell us what's the craic, who slept with who?"

"Well I don't know if they slept together, but they definitely left together," I tease.

"Ooh, intriguing," Graham says, his face lighting up and him and his box shuffling closer.

"And they left pretty early too so I can only assume." I add.

"Who? Who?" Jerry begs now.

"You, know Kate?" I say, enjoying the mini power trip.

Taylor, cleaning the galley tops, 'the cleaners don't do it properly' she always says, turns her head to join in but keeps cleaning. "Oh I love Kate; she's such a sweet heart."

"Yeah she is. But you'll never guess who she left with." I drag out my pause while they all wait, watching me. "Pervert Pete!"

"No way!" Graham and Jerry say in unison.

"Oh no, she's far too sweet for him. What was she thinking?" Taylor asks, mostly to herself.

"Feck off, no she didn't." Jerry says to me playfully.

"She fecking did. Saw it with my own eyes," I tell them. "We tried to stop her, but she was having none of it."

"Oh sweet Jaysus, why?" Jerry asks, as if I know the answer. All I can do is answer with a shrug.

"Well that poor girl is not living that down for a while. Not while I'm around," Graham says wiggling his finger and pursing his lips.

"So who else was out?" Jerry interrupts Graham's judgement.

"Oh well, Jack, who was so, so drunk, it was hilarious, Will, Ant, Ian," I try to say his name as quickly as possible, "Kaylee, absolutely loving life, and Suzi, coming on to every guy she saw."

"Really?" Taylor asks. She's braved the toilets once more and is now re-stocking them.

"Stripe chaser!" Graham shouts.

"Don't make me laugh." Jerry says whilst ignoring his own words and giggling again.

"A what?" Taylor asks.

"Stripe chaser! You know the stripes on a pilot's uniform? Yeah, well some girls are only interested in money and a man to look after them. The more stripes, the better," Graham informs her.

"Oh I see," she says. I can see the cogs in her brain going round as she processes this.

"Any ol' pilot or just any ol' man?" Jerry asks.

"Seemed to be pilots last night, but could just be because it was crew night." I say, and then wonder why I'm letting her off. It *was* pilots and specifically Ian.

"Like a flight deck floozy then?" Taylor asks, just catching up on the conversation.

"Same thing," Jerry tells her. "What pilots were out then? Ian?"

Damn, didn't say it quick enough. Although it's stupid trying to hide it, there'll be pictures up all over the internet by now. "Yeah, Ian, and a friend of his from flight school."

Graham interrupts me. "I don't like Ian."

This takes me back a bit.

"Why?" Taylor asks and he and Jerry share a knowing glance.

"Oh he's lovely to you girls; he's just not a massive fan of us gays. Just 'cos we're not flirting with him or talking about football he doesn't seem to really bother. So I don't bother with him," Graham says.

Taylor looks at me and I look to Jerry for confirmation.

"Too true," Jerry shakes his head. "I don't particularly like flying with him."

I try to hide my shock. I feel like I should be sticking up for him, he's just quiet and keeps himself to himself, even when you know him well. But I can't. Can't let them know I care. Take the subject off him.

"Well I can only say what I saw, and Suzi seemed to want to get to know Ian's friend very personally, touching his arm, dancing well grinding on him." That's it, throw her under the bus to save yourself. "He bought her drinks all night."

"I guess we'll just have to keep our ears open for the next instalment. More from galley FM next Thursday," Graham says with a wink as he holds his hands up to his mouth, imitating a microphone. We all laugh, but underneath I'm screaming shhhiiiittttttt!! Why did I open my mouth?

"Best go check on the boys, so I should." Jerry says and makes his way up to the front of the cabin.

MUC

The Cockpit Voice Recorder CVR or 'Black Box' as it is commonly known, records all sounds in the cockpit and all radio transmissions for a minimum of 30 minutes, on a loop. It is in fact bright orange, so that it will stand out in a crash. The recordings take place in case of an emergency landing and so the inspectors can find out what happened in those last crucial moments. However, there are thousands of flights that happen every day without a hitch and thousands of conversations for which the voice recorder is there for throughout.

CAM - Cockpit area microphone voice or sound source

HOT - Flight crew audio panel voice or sound source

RDO - Radio transmissions from Air Traffic Control

-1 Voice identified as the captain

-2 Voice identified as the first officer

-3 Voice identified as the cabin crew

Expletive

* Unintelligible

… Pause

20:02:16 CAM – [Door beep and click as it opens]

20:02:24 HOT – 3 - Tea, milk, no sugar, for you Ryan.

20:02:28 HOT – 2 - Thank you darlin'.

20:02:30 HOT – 3 - Coffee, black, and a bacon butty for you Ian. Ketchup?

20: 02:36 HOT – 1 - Oh, umm.

20:02:39 HOT – 2 - [Laughter]

20:02:43 HOT – 3 - It's only my stocking Ian. I don't have any pockets on my uniform and I can't carry everything in my hands and open the door. Quite useful don't you think? [Laughter]. I'll get it then, honestly, pilots are so lazy, you can't even get your own ketchup.

20:03:04 HOT – 1 - * It's in your stocking.

20:03:08 HOT – 3 - Yes Ian, I just explained that to you.

20:03:11 HOT – 2 - [Still laughing]

20:03:15 HOT – 3 - Can I get you anything else?

20:03:18 HOT – 2 - No thanks doll, I'm fine.

20:03:21 CAM – [Rustling]

20:03:23 HOT – 3 - Ok. Oh yeah, guess who's sitting down the back with a baseball cap over their face and a strop on?

20:03:30 HOT – 2 - Who?

20:03:33 HOT – 3 - Tara Day.

20:03:35 HOT – 2 - Awesome.

20:03: 37 HOT – 1 - Who?

20:03: 39 HOT – 3 - From that film, A Zeal of Zebras, the blonde one.

20:03:44 HOT – 2 - Big jugs.

20:03:46 HOT – 1 - Oh really?

20:03: 48 HOT – 3 - [Laughter] Jugs? Oh Ryan. They're not that big.

20:03:51 HOT – 2 - They're not small. [Laughter]

20:03: 55 HOT – 1 - Well you can invite her into the cockpit when we land if you like.

20:04:01 HOT – 3 - Ask her yourself.

20:04:04 HOT – 1 - Ok, well can you tell Neil we'll be landing in to Munich in about twenty minutes.

20:04:09 HOT – 3 - Will do.

20:04:12 CAM – [Door click, opens and door slam, closes.]

20:04:20 HOT – 1 - That girl.

20:04:22 HOT – 2 - What Tara Day? [Laughter]

20:04:26 HOT – 1 - No Kaylee.

20:04:29 HOT – 2 - She just doesn't give a #, I love it.

20:04: 32 HOT – 1 – Don't encourage her, you'll set the cabin crew gay mafia off as well.

20:04:37 HOT – 2 – Excuse me?

20:04:41 HOT – 1 – You know what I mean.

20:04:43 HOT – 2 – Actually I don't…

20:04:45 HOT – 1 – Well…

20:04:46 HOT – 2- But being gay myself maybe I'm just confused?

20:04:50 HOT – 1 - # [Coughs].

30:04:54 CAM – [Rustling].

20:04:57 HOT – 1 – Sorry *.

20:05:00 HOT – 2 – Uh huh.

20:05:02 HOT – 1 – No really * I'm sorry.

20:05:06 HOT – 2 – Let's change the subject shall we?

20:05:10 HOT – 1 - So… would you mind if I say goodbye to the passengers as they leave?

20:05:17 HOT – 2 - You're the boss.

20:05:21 HOT – 1 - So she's fit then, Tara Day?

20:05:24 HOT – 2 - She's hot yeah. I wanna meet her too, so invite her in. We'll get pictures.

20:05:29 HOT – 1 - Yeah… Ok.

20:14:01 HOT – 2 - …So are you still living in a hotel?

20:14:06 HOT – 1 - No, I found a house, so I'm just renting at the moment.

20:14:10 HOT – 2 – Are you living with anyone?

20:14:13 HOT – 1 - No, no. I decided I'm better on my own.

20:14:18 HOT – 2 - Fair, and how's your girlfriend?

20:14:21 HOT – 1 - We broke up actually, last week.

20:14:25 HOT – 2 - Ah #, I'm sorry.

20:14:27 HOT – 1 - No it's ok. It wasn't really working.

20:14:31 HOT – 2 - Still, I'm sorry.

20:14:34 HOT – 1 - … I'm actually quite happy about it.

20:14:40 HOT – 2 - …Ok.

20:14:43 HOT – 1 - No, I just mean… it was hard work and it's best for both of us you know.

20:14:49 HOT – 2 - Yeah, relationships are hard, man. Only you know when to draw the line.

20:14:56 HOT – 1 - Yes, exactly… I also started seeing someone else.

20:15:02 HOT - 2 - That does help.

20:15:05 HOT – 1 - She's just easy you know.

20:15:08 HOT – 2 - Oh really?

20:15:10 HOT – 1 - I mean it's easy. We're on the same page, it's just sex.

20:15:15 HOT – 2 - Oh, friends with benefits, nice.

20:15:18 HOT – 1 - Is that kind of what it's like being gay? Lots of friends with benefits?

20:15:23 HOT – 2 - [Laughter] Well it's the same as being straight. Some people like relationships and some don't.

20:15:31 HOT – 1 - But I mean, men are on the same page, we all just want to get laid. Right?

20:15:37 HOT – 2 - It is kind of a thing in gay culture, yeah. I know what you mean. But still, it's just up to the individual person.

20:15:46 HOT – 1 - Of course.

20:15:48 HOT – 2 - Sounds like, you're interested?

20:15:51 CAM – [Splutters] *.

20:15:55 HOT – 2 - That wasn't an invitation don't worry.

20:15:59 HOT – 1 – Umm… well… I'm quite happy with Charlie for now.

20:16:05 HOT – 2 - Charlie? As in Charlie who works here?

20:16:09 HOT – 1 - Oh #. * I shouldn't have said that…

20:16:14 HOT – 2 - Don't worry, it's ok.

20:16:17 HOT – 1 - I mean we're not really telling people… I mean it's not even a real thing so you know.

20:16:25 HOT – 2 - It's fine man, don't worry about it. I'm not gunna tell anyone.

20:16:30 HOT – 1 - #, thank you.

20:16:33 HOT – 2 - I mean the biggest gossip here already knows, right?

20:16:37 HOT – 1 - What?

20:16:39 HOT – 2 - Charlie. She already knows.

20:16:43 HOT – 1 - What? *

20:16:46 HOT – 2 - I'm sure your secret's safe.

20:16:50 RDO – Almond 879 descend to altitude 5000ft, GNH 1007

20:16:54 HOT – 1 - Descend to altitude 5000ft, GNH 1007, Almond 879

20:17:00 HOT – 2 - Set QNH please

20:17:03 HOT – 1 - 1007 set and cross-checked

20:17:07 HOT – 2 - Descent mode engaged

20:17:09 HOT – 1 - Alt blue, 5000ft checks

20:17:13 HOT – 2 - Approach checklist please

20:17:15 CAM – [Rustling]

20:17:22 HOT – 1 - Approach checklist… briefing?

20:17:26 HOT – 2 - Confirmed for runway 28

20:17:30 HOT – 1 - ECAM status?

20:17:33 HOT – 2 - Checked

20:17:36 HOT – 1 - Seat belts?

20:17:38 HOT – 2 - On.

20:17:41 HOT – 1 - Baro?

20:17:44 HOT – 2 - 1007 set both sides

20:17:47 HOT – 1 - MDA?

20:17:51 HOT – 2 - 400ft set

20:17:54 HOT – 1 - Engine mode select?

20:17:57 HOT – 2 - Normal

20:17:59 HOT – 1 - Approach checks complete

20:18:01 HOT – 2 - Thank you kindly.

VIE

"Suzi, Suzi," Ben calls over to me, as I approach him he grabs my arm and whispers in my ear, "I feel like everyone's watching me."

I look around to try and see if his statement is true; everyone's chatting and yes it does seem a few people are looking at us; as I meet their eyes they smile weakly. Pathetic. If they have something to say to Ben, then just say it. I project this thought at them with my eyes squinted, then realise they're not looking any more. In fact Liam seems to be trying really hard to look anywhere but at us. Yep, pathetic.

I can't believe that Kath, Base Manager of all people, would put Ben in this position: outing him so he feels scared of coming to work. He should feel safe here, with people who call themselves his friends.

The crew room is busy as people on early flights have returned, with bags under their eyes, and crew members like me and Ben are arriving for late flights, also with bags under our eyes. Somehow the crew on lates, including myself, look wearier than those on earlies; it's because we know we're only just starting and they know they're going home.

"They're not looking at you, don't worry," I answer, "and if anyone does say anything then just tell them to fuck off, sweetie." I really should stop swearing at work, it's going to slip out in front of a passenger onc day.

"I'm just glad Kath has gone home already," Ben says; the thought had already entered my mind as we entered the crew room.

"Yeah, lazy shit. But you know you're going to have to see her at some point," I reply.

"I know, but I will avoid her for as long as I possibly can," he adds with a smile.

"I think I'm going to have to avoid her as well, just so I don't get in trouble for punching her in the face."

Ben laughs at this but I'm serious.

"I'm very tempted."

"Talking of wanting to avoid people," Ben nods his head towards Josh who is coming our way.

"Hey!" Josh calls as he makes his way over to us. He kisses me on both cheeks and then kisses Ben on both cheeks. This is a tad awkward.

"We're flying together on Monday," Josh says, directing his attention towards me.

"Are we? Awesome. Who else are we with?"

"Charlie and Gabriella, nice little crew. So did you have fun at crew night the other night?"

"Yeah it was alright. Same as usual."

"I heard you ended up in my boyfriend's bed, yet again." Josh says laughing. "If I didn't know better I'd say you were trying to turn him." I hear Ben next to me make a choking sound which he tries to turn into a laugh, I join in and after a glance in Ben's direction Josh does too.

"We both know how much Jack loves boobs, but there is no way he'd leave the cock alone," I say almost whispering the last bit, not wanting to shout 'cock' across the crew room. "And besides he's far too greedy."

"Or is that just your cover story? Was it someone else's bed you ended up in?" Josh asks with a wink.

"Unfortunately, having the duvet stolen off of me and almost being pushed out of bed by your boyfriend is as close as I got to sleeping with a man," I tell him.

"Oh god, tell me about it. That's why I leave him to it when he's drunk," he says, but I wonder if that's the real reason or not.

I look at Josh, his smiling face, everyone loves him; he and Jack are the star couple at the base. How different it would be if everyone else knew about Jack and Ben? I remember accidentally seeing their first kiss, Jack and Ben's that is, how cute it was, how romantic, until I remembered the boyfriend, Josh. I felt guilty just watching. Apparently Jack and Ben didn't feel the same way. I always wonder if Josh knows, and what he'd do if he found out I'd known all along. Not much, he's not vicious. But I knew

Jack first, and I can't help but stay loyal to his cheating arse.

As Josh talks I feel Ben beside me slip away, and out the corner of my eye I see him quickly join another conversation, I don't know if Josh notices or cares; he doesn't seem to. I tune back into what Josh is saying as he's shuffling his paperwork like a news reader.

"Anyways, best do my briefing, checking in in a minute. So I'll see you Monday," he says with a warm smile and another two kisses on my cheeks.

"Will do, have a good flight."

"With the stuck up bastards of Nice? I doubt it," he says as he walks away.

I check in myself and check my drop file. I don't really expect to see anything in there but you never know when you've had a few days off. Usually it's just someone putting shit in your drop file, like fifty sachets of ketchup. Usually it's Jack.

I head over to the cabin crew instructions and memos; the only new one is that we are out of stock of bacon butties. Damn it, I really fancied one! Oh well I'm sure there are a few left over biccies in the kitchen. I check my watch. There's still time before I check in, so a brew and some biscuits it is.

As I enter the kitchen talking away to myself, muttering under my breath. I see him suddenly before me. I jump and then he jumps and then I jump again.

"Shit! You just scared the life out of me!"

It's one of the new captains, over from another base, but I can't remember which base, or what his name is. I realise I've just screamed in his face so try to smile politely as I make my way into the kitchen properly.

"Sorry Suzi, I scared myself too."

Shit he knows my name, and I really can't remember his. I'm sure I've only seen him once in passing. I try to wing it. "Hey, how are you?"

"Good thank you, now my heart rate has settled."

I laugh at his joke, maybe a little too much, really what is his name? I try to place his bald head, his broad shoulders, his cheeky smile. In his pilot uniform he looks respectable; in certain other clothes he could look quite scary, threatening even.

"You caught me red handed." He holds up the jar of the good coffee. "We've run out in the pilot's room." He pretends to look guilty.

"Oh I see. I was just in my own little world."

"Would you like a cup of tea or coffee?"

"A pilot making the drinks? Not seen that before." He laughs at my sarcasm. I'm still trying to work him out. Is he a Michael... Mark? I just can't think. "Coffee please, two sugars."

"Coming right up," he says, putting the kettle on.

The door swings open and in walks Laura.

"Mason, how are you?" She steps straight past me and kisses his cheek.

Mason that's it, I was close.

"Good thank you." He beams back at her, with his cheeky smile. "And yourself, Lovely Laura?"

"All the better for seeing you, my darling," she says, washing her mug in the sink and leaving it on the drying rack.

They talk as if each of them couldn't be any more pleased to see another person. What's going on? Did I just forget to pay attention to the whole base for like, a month? How does he know everyone? I keep smiling my stupid, confused smile.

"See you later darling," Laura says to Mason blowing a kiss to him over her shoulder. "Oh Suzi. Hi," she adds, and then leaves.

Is it me or was that a tad… rude?

He looks at me, I look at him.

"So I'm not in her best books apparently," I try to say with a laugh.

He smiles back at me, but something's not quite right. Does he look embarrassed?

"I'm sure it's nothing," I add trying to work out the look on his face.

"I think," he coughs, straightening his jacket and not quite looking me in the eye, "I think you should maybe know," Mason says.

"Know what?"

"Well, I mean it's not really any of my business."

"No, go on."

"There are some rumours going round the pilot's crew room and they've come from the cabin crew so I'm guessing a few people here have heard them."

"Ok," I say. "I'm not exactly sure what this has to do with me." Does he want me to validate them or something?

"They're about you."

"Oh." So yes, he does want me to validate them. "Are you sure? My life really isn't that interesting."

"I'm sure it's nothing, I just thought you should be aware people are talking about you." He gestures towards the closed door, after Laura.

"What are they saying then?"

He does an uncomfortable shuffle, I notice his belly hanging over his trousers slightly and realise his broad shoulders aren't muscle. How old is he, thirty, thirty five, forty maybe?

"Well I heard that you were stripe chasing… at crew night."

"What the fuck? Who told you that?" I almost shout, and then try and compose myself.

"It's just what a few people have said." He blushes as the kettle boils and concentrates on making our drinks. "Laura said, that Graham was told by Charlie…"

"Well it's a load of bollocks, so there you go, there's your answer," I say defensively. Laura? Graham? Charlie? Charlie was at crew night with me and Jack. How dare she?

"I didn't mean to upset you," he says, handing me my coffee. "Biscuit?" He opens the biscuit drawer, all of a sudden looking childlike, the way bald men sometimes do - like a baby.

I laugh, more naturally this time.

"So who did I sleep with then? Any one in particular or am I just letting everyone have a go?"

"Well, what I heard was that you had a soft spot for Ian. Do you know Ian?"

"I know Ian, but really?" I feel a little bit sick. "Just – no!"

He laughs, I guess at the look of horror on my face. "Well the rumour says you had a soft spot for Ian until his friend arrived."

I try to remember his friend. God, I really need to start paying attention to pilots, seeing as I'm supposedly sleeping with them. Ian's friend finally pops into my head. "Oh god, him! No, no, no. I mean yeah I was drunk and having a little dance, but I was not *that* drunk."

"I know you're not like that. I just thought you should know."

"Thanks." There's a moment of silence where we stare at each other. I take a sip of my drink as I can't think of anything else to say. He does the same. "I best go. Don't want to be late for my briefing," I say.

"Well I'm your captain so I'll just tell your senior, who is it, Luke, that he can fuck off if he says anything," he says, with a smug look on his face.

"I'll hold you to that," I reply.

I walk back through the crew room slightly dazed. I look for Ben and realise he's watching me with a grin on his face.

"What's happened to you?" he asks me.

"I don't know. I'm confused."

"Sorry guys but its ten to, can we start our briefing?" Luke asks, all of a sudden by my side, making me jump yet again.

We move over to a small, cornered off table and I try my hardest to listen to the briefing: passenger numbers, flight times, service. Have I got my ID, passport, green card? Yes. I absentmindedly answer the safety and security questions; where are the oxygen bottles and masks on board? What do we do if we lose pressure in the cabin? How do we treat a sprain or strain?

"RICE," I hear my voice shout, "Rest, Ice, Compression, Elevation." I sound like a robot, going through the motions.

All I can think of, however, are Mason's words. I look up at Jessica sat next to me, she catches my eye and looks away quickly, staring intently at her hands clasped on her lap. Was Ben right? Maybe everyone was staring, just not at him. Shit. Do people really believe these rumours? Laura, Jessica, Liam. They know me; they know I'm not fucking around. But they do believe them, they believe Charlie. And I thought finally I was fitting in, like I was finally good at something.

As we leave the crew room and head for the aircraft I have Ben at my side. In unison we step, left, right, left, right and drag our wheelie cases behind us.

"So what happened back there? You came out of the kitchen with some weird look on your face," says Ben.

We try to talk quietly, but crossing the tarmac is always a challenge, with planes rolling past, and baggage carts trying to run us over or attack us with loose, flying baggage. I tell him about what happened in the kitchen. I tell him everything: about Mason, and not really knowing who he was; about Laura and the weird look of disapproval on her face when she saw me; about the rumours, about Ian and about Charlie.

We're silent for a while both mulling over our own thoughts. The air around us hums with the songs of aircraft, coming and going, people coming and going.

I think back to before I was flying, before I even knew what a galley was. Back to when I was dancing and one of the reasons I was happy to be able to get out of that world was because of the bitching and back stabbing. It seems to have followed me, yet again. I thought I was entering a whole new world, of beaches and sunshine and amazing memories. Now I can barely remember yesterday, the days blur into one as I jet back and forth to places, never seeing past the airport. Living the dream, eh.

Ben interrupts my musings. "Jessica already told me."

"What?" I don't mean to but my feet stop walking. "So you already knew?"

63

"Yeah, come on," he grabs my arms and leads me forward this time; "I just wanted to know your gossip before I told you mine."

"But your gossip is my gossip."

"And I thought everyone was going to be talking about me."

"Yeah, you're welcome."

"Sorry, look I told Jessica it was bollocks. And she can go and tell people its bollocks. And your new best friend, Mr Captain, can go and tell everyone its bollocks so don't worry." Ben reassures me, a smile beaming across his face, now the tables have turned and I'm the one in the limelight. Although, from the look on Jessica's face in the briefing I don't think she believed him.

Dragging behind, we see the rest of the crew reach the plane. Mason lets Luke and Jessica up the stairs first then gestures to us and shouts, "hurry up," with a laugh.

We take a little trot, pretending to speed up then fall back into our steady walk. Ben takes a long look at Mason.

"Why's he so interested anyway?" he asks.

"That's what I was wondering. I really don't know."

"Maybe he really is just being nice, and we're just being cynical."

"Maybe." I hadn't thought of that.

As we reach the plane Mason is still waiting for us. He lets us up the stairs before him, Ben goes first but as I pass him he grabs hold of my wheelie case. Despite my protests, he insists and follows up the stairs behind me. It's quite unnecessary as my bag is light and it's completely out of the ordinary for a captain to think of the cabin crew before themselves.

On the aircraft I follow Ben down the back of the aircraft to start our safety and security checks. Over the PA Mason's voice booms out, full of self-assurance.

"Any requests?"

"What?" Ben asks me and I shrug my shoulders.

A moment later a guitar starts playing, we both stop walking and look around. The music comes over the PA system, loud yet beautiful. I look back down the aisle and see Mason, his head peering out of the cockpit, holding his mobile phone up to the PA phone with a smile on his face. He winks at me. I quickly look away and inadvertently catch Luke's eye. His shoulders have tensed up. Bless him, he's a sweethcart really but a little bit anal. This music must be killing him; this is not how things are done.

We continue to make our way down the aisle, unpack our things and start our checks. I listen to the strumming and picking of the guitar, the melody relaxing me, taking my suspicious, questioning thoughts away. I could get used to working like this.

The flight is normal, no more comments, or gossip, or random songs playing down the PA. Although Ben and I do have a small…ish food fight in the back galley on the flight home.

It's just easy working with Ben. Some people might say that this job is easy; they'd be wrong. Some people might say you can't be good or bad at this job, but again they'd be wrong. Ben is just so good at his job. I'm kind of jealous.

As we disembark the passengers I hear Ben in the office, more commonly known as the toilet, on the phone arranging to meet Jack.

"Bye, bye. Thank you. Safe journey home." I say to the passengers.

Ben whispers in my ear. "I'm going to stay at Jack's tonight. That ok?"

"Yeah sure. Do you want a lift? Bye, bye. Thank you."

"No I'll get the train, got spare clothes in my case."

The last passenger gets off and we grab our bags and high-vis and run to the front.

All of a sudden Ben is in front of me talking to Ashleah, the FO. Luke and Jessica are in front still, chatting away, and I notice Mason is by my side, taking my crew case from me and carrying it whilst conducting a full blown conversation that I didn't know had started. I feel bad: pay attention.

"...so we're moving in in a week, me and Ron, the missus is still up North. It's right next to the train station but for now it's back to the hotel and spending money on trains and taxis, eating out and washing my clothes. I can't wait to just be settled here."

Shit, pretend you were listening. "I know exactly what you mean."

Back in the crew room, Ben asks the questions I should probably have been asking. "How are you finding it here Mason? Have you been to crew night yet? Where are you staying? Oh that's right near Suzi's place."

Mason looks at me with a smile and pleading eyes. "I couldn't bother you for a lift could I? The next train's not for another forty minutes."

What can I say? Fuck off?

I don't, of course, and before I know it I'm in my car, no Ben, no crew, no crew room just me and Mason. And he's talking again, he asked a question, I think.

"Sorry, what?"

"What's your story? What did you do before flying?"

"Oh. No story really. I'm not that interesting."

"I'm sure you are. Did you always want to fly?"

"No. I kind of fell into it actually. I just seemed to get to a point in my life where a lot of the people I knew were either pilots or cabin crew, and I thought, that sounds fun."

He laughs at this and I take my eyes off the road to look at him. I didn't expect him to be looking back. I laugh along with him, although I wasn't trying to be funny. I think he's just one of those people who laugh at anything and everything, that's just how they react. 'Mason, your dog just died.' 'Ha ha!'

"What did you want to do then? What was your dream?"

I can feel my cheeks turn red, although I don't usually blush. I realise it's because of the person asking the question not the question itself. It feels weird telling an almost stranger what your dreams are, were. I feel the words forming and against my better judgement I tell him anyway.

"I wanted to be a dancer."

"Why didn't you?"

"I wasn't good enough."

"I'm sure that's not true." He nudges my knee in encouragement.

"No it's true." This time we both laugh. "I was good, just not good enough. That and by the time I was eighteen my body was already starting to fall apart."

"You seem pretty intact to me." His eyes linger over my body just a little too long.

"Yeah on the outside sure; on the inside my joints are well and truly fucked. So I was looking for something else to do. Did a few random jobs here and there and then this came up."

That last statement isn't completely true. I had lots of different jobs between leaving college and starting flying but they were just filling time. Whilst everyone else was getting ready for university at the age of eighteen, I was applying for dance school. And every audition I went to I saw someone better than me. That's not me being self-deprecating that's just fact.

After each audition I would get a letter through the post. My heart wouldn't just flutter it would be ready to fly away and I'd open the letter as quick as a flick to read, 'blah, blah, blah, thank you for auditioning, blah, blah, blah, unfortunately this time you were unsuccessful'. Unfortunately. And my heart would sink back down into my body and lie there, barely beating. After the first few rejections, I kept going. The letters kept coming and I kept reading 'unfortunately this time you were unsuccessful.' It got harder with each letter I ripped open until eventually I just looked for that word, unfortunately, and every time, it was there.

Before I knew it auditions were over and my friends were all starting university. I got a job, here, there and everywhere. It didn't matter, because next year I would be better, I would be more prepared. Next year I would get in. And next year came. Again I started off with high hopes and soon they came crashing down around me, once again. Another year over. Another whole year to wait till next time.

The third year I decided was my last. If I didn't get in, it just wasn't meant to be. Something bigger and better was just around the corner. I tried, I really did. But, unfortunately, I didn't get in.

So I decided I needed a break; from dance, from anything creative. I decided I needed a proper job. Well I wouldn't say flying was a 'proper job'. But it pays the bills. Just.

I don't say any of that to Mason, however, I just smile.

"And you like flying?"

"Yeah. It'll do. Here we go."

We pull up outside his hotel. Half-eleven and its quiet. One smoker standing out the front trying not to stare into the gaze of my headlights, puffs away.

I look over to Mason who's looking back, closer than I thought.

"Thank you," he says, quieter than his usual commanding manner. I can feel his breath on my face. And then he kisses me.

He kisses me. Hard, wet. His tongue pushes its way through and that's when I pull away. I look at him, waiting for an apology but he kisses me again. This time I push as hard as I can on his chest to get him away; my push isn't that strong but he relinquishes his hold.

"What the fuck are you doing?" I ask, pressing myself against my door, trying to get as far away from him as possible.

"I'm sorry..."

"You have a girlfriend."

"I'm sorry. You're just so beautiful. The first time I saw you I was in awe and flying with you today... I'm sorry." His thoughts trail off and he mumbles, "you're just so beautiful."

I take a deep breath and in as strong a voice as I can muster I say, "I think you should leave, now."

He places his hand on my knee and starts to say something but I shout this time, "Now!"

He nods his head, removes his hand and opens the door. Once outside he bends down to look back into the car.

"Please, forgive me," he begs and closes the door.

I watch him enter the hotel and wait for his silhouette and presence to fade. I drive off as fast as I can, wiping the feel of his mouth from mine, tears beginning to fall down my cheeks.

ZRH

Iza wakes with a start. Her curtains, slightly parted, throw a slither of early morning sunshine across her bed. She squints and looks for the time: 8:11am her phone reads, four hours before she needs to get up but alcohol always does that to her, it always gets her up early. One new message flashes on her phone. It's from Ali. I'll read it in a minute, she thinks as she closes her eyes.

She tries to remember her dream but all she can gather together is the fear, the tightness in her chest, her hands desperately trying to hold onto something. Giving up she opens her eyes again. Her feet find their way out of bed and into slippers and in her pyjamas she leaves her room.

In the kitchen she boils the kettle and makes herself a cup of tea. An almost empty wine glass, flanked by an empty wine bottle sits on the counter top, the smell of the alcohol drifts towards her, making her want to leave the room as soon as possible.

"Oh God," she says under her breath.

She grabs a pair of sunglasses, a packet of cigarettes and heads out the front door.

Outside the air is just warming up. Iza sits on the top step that leads up to her block of flats. She takes out a cigarette, lights it and relaxes back onto the front door. She takes a drag of nicotine, takes a sip of tea and then gets her phone out to read Ali's message.

Hey babe. One more week to go! I can't friggin wait to be back home with you; putting my feet up, watching the tele and cuddling you all night. Flights are all booked. I get back to you in the early hours of the 15th so I can take my wonderful girlfriend out for lunch and then we can go back to bed... for a nap ☺ Mum's got the spare bedroom all ready for us on the 22nd. Are you sure you're ok to drive all the way up to Leeds? We can always get the train, just need to book tickets. It would be better if we drove just so we can get around town and get out of it as well. But no biggie. Anyways, I'm off to work now, I know you start just as I finish so maybe just send me a little message for me to come back to and fingers crossed I'll talk to you tomorrow. I love you soooooooo much. Not long now ☺ Ali xxxxxxxxxxxxxxxxxxxxxxxx

His message is soppy as usual. If his friends back home knew how he talked to her they wouldn't be able to control their laughter. If her parents knew, back in Poland, they'd say 'this is what you get for choosing an English man'. But she likes it, she needs it, she needs to know that he finds it hard too, that he misses her just as much as she misses him, otherwise she'd explode. She thinks how these past five weeks have dragged and her heart feels heavy. So heavy it sinks down into her stomach and crushes her insides.

Everyone at work asked how it was going to work. Him in Shanghai, her still here, getting on with things. She told them it'd be fine, she was prepared for it to be hard, to work hard at it. He was only going to be gone for six weeks at a time and then she'd have him all to herself for two weeks. That last part wasn't quite true. He always wanted to see his family, especially his mum, and his friends too. Of course he would, she never stopped him. But she felt jealous all the same.

She knew it would be hard. She just didn't realise that every time she had to say goodbye, every time he left, it would get harder. She wasn't prepared for that. The days exaggerated, the weeks extending into what seems like forever and a day, until the next time she gets to see him.

Over the road a door opens and out of it Jack appears, a black bag full of rubbish in his hand as he happily jumps down the steps. Putting the bag in the wheelie bin he notices Iza over the road and waves a hello. She reciprocates, cigarette in hand.

"Hang on I'll join you," he shouts across the road, "let me just get my fags." And with that he bounces back up the stairs into the building.

The chase between Iza and Ali had been long, on and off and on again, until Ali made her an ultimatum and Iza realised she didn't want to let him go. He hadn't told her about Shanghai then. How he'd already applied for the job, to pay off the debt of his flight training he said, and then later he would add, 'and to buy us a nice house, for our kids and our dogs.' Yes it was early on in their relationships to be making those kinds of statements but they only made

Iza believed this was the real thing even more. Now she wonders if they would have been together in the first place if he'd told her straight away that all he was waiting for was the final 'yes' from recruitment and he'd be gone, out of England, for two years.

Two years is not so bad, Iza told herself. It's not so bad if when he gets back we can really set up our life together. Now a year later Iza isn't sure what that life means? Another ultimatum from Ali: 'I want to move to Edinburgh,' and she doesn't know what she wants. But she does know she has no friends, no family, no job in Edinburgh and that she doesn't want to be cabin crew any more. She's sick of passengers thinking they're above the cabin crew, that as crew you're just some stupid bimbo, that her foreign accent makes her stupid. She knows now she wants to train to be something more, something more important. And she's had her final 'yes'. She's in.

Jack bounds back out of his house and jogs over to where Iza is sitting. She shuffles over to make room for him and without even thinking gives him the obligatory two kisses on each cheek. He picks the lighter up that was sat next to Iza.

"You ok?" he asks with his first intake of smoke.

"You know how you wake up and everything is lovely; the sun is shining, the birds are singing, then a second later you remember how shit life is?" Iza croaks out, realising how angry she sounds and wishing she didn't.

"Yep! Know that feeling only too well," Jack replies, taking another drag.

"It's like ahhh, I'm awake, I'm alive, I'm healthy. And in a few hours I have to go and be physically and mentally abused by some random people who call themselves passengers. I call them *dupkami* but you know."

Jack looks at her with a raised eyebrow.

"That means assholes in Polish," she explains and they laugh together.

"D*upkami*, I like it," Jack says with a smile, repeating it over again to himself.

Jack looks at Iza, her face pale, her eyes dark-ringed from lack of sleep.

"You sure there isn't anything else bothering you?"

"Just a stress dream," Iza replies.

"You sure?"

Iza looks down at her feet not sure how much to say to Jack, if she should say anything at all.

"Anything to do with Ali?" Jack asks.

"That obvious?" Iza asks, looking into his sincere face.

He smiles at her and as she sighs she lets it all out.

"He says that *we* can be happy in Edinburgh, that *we* should move there, but how? Originally the plan was for him to be back in a year, there's no point me being over there, or so he says, and when he comes back we were going to find a place here. But I guess we've both messed that up now."

"How have you messed that up?" Jack asks, looking confused.

"Well I applied to become a paramedic. And I got onto the course. I heard a few days ago."

"Wow!" Jack shouts and hugs her tight. "That's fantastic!"

Iza falls into his embrace, enjoying the moment, celebrating her success, something she hasn't let herself do yet.

"Where is the training? When does it start?" Jack asks, excited for her.

"London, September," Iza replies, and with those words the sudden excitement she enjoyed is gone.

"Oh, and he wants you to be in Edinburgh, I see." His face falls.

They sit in silence for a minute, one of Jack's arms still around Iza.

"So he has to go where the jobs are. And if you want to be with him, you have to go too?" he asks.

"Yeah. But I just keep thinking, what about my job? What about training?" Iza asks, a tear in her eye.

"That's the way it is when your boyfriend is a pilot. You follow him. You do what he wants," Jack says, though he isn't happy with what he has to say.

"What about me?" Iza asks. "I can't do what I want?"

"Of course you can," Jack replies. "But.."

"But?" Iza ask desperately.

"I guess you have to choose who you love more, Ali or yourself?" he replies and then falls silent. They sit on the step, unable to make eye contact.

Iza sniffs not bothering to hide her tears. Why should she?

"What would you do, if Josh was a pilot, if he earned five times as much as you and he asked you to move to a different city?" she asks looking at him and sees the cogs turning behind his eyes, into his brain.

He thinks for a while and tries to find the right thing to say but then he realises he has no idea. What would he do? Would he give up his life here? Would Josh support his life style? Would he expect Josh to? Is it all about money? Because it really should be about love, about the relationship, about two people starting their life together but is it? What would people expect of him, his family, his friends? He suspects they wouldn't be as shocked if he said no to Josh than if Iza said no to Ali but why? Because he's a man? He's allowed to think for himself?

He thinks of his relationship with Josh, what is their plan? Do they have to have one? Why all of a sudden does it have to become so serious? He thinks how lucky he is that Josh is happy and settled just how they are. It's easy. It just, kind of, works.

He looks at Iza, her expectant eyes waiting for him to give her the answer. But all he can think of is, "I don't know."

His cigarette burns his fingertips and he lets it drop to the floor.

Iza sits on the edge of her bed in her ironed uniform. Her hair perfect in its bun, her fringe just above her eyebrows, no longer; small pearl earrings sit in her ears; her make-up immaculate, red lip stick and long eye lashes; her nails flawlessly manicured; her watch, not too flashy, not too dull, ticks by on her wrist. Her laptop sits on her legs, her finger hovering, waiting to click send. She reads her message one more time.

Hey honey. I hope work is going ok, I'm just about to leave but wanted to say a quick hello.

So a while ago I told you that I was thinking about applying to train as a paramedic but I didn't know if I'd get in, or if my application was too late, but all I really knew was that I just can't fly any more. I don't want to be stuck with no qualifications, miserable, in this job for the rest of my life.

Well it turns out I wasn't too late to apply, or too stupid. I got in. It's one of the best courses in the country for grades and jobs afterwards. It's only an hour away from where I'm living now so even if I do move I'll still be close for when you get back. We'll both be set for jobs and we can start our life together.

Have a think about it and I'll talk to you tomorrow. I love you so so so so so so much and I cannot wait for this week to be over, it's going so slowly. See you soon XXXXXXXX

Iza looks at her watch, she has to leave for work now or she'll be late. Her hand shakes. She presses send and reminds herself to breathe.

Grabbing her handbag and wheelie case, she puts her heels on and head for the door.

Outside she sees Jack again talking to someone in their car, she can't see who. He stands up straight and shouts over to her.

"Hey Iza, come over later if you want, when you finish work, I'll still be up."

"Ok," she shouts back but she's not sure if she will.

As she gets into her car parked out the front the flats her phone buzzes. It's a message from Ali.

What about Edinburgh?

81

All day at work, from when she checks in to when she checks out, Iza thinks about that message. It floats in front of her eyes as if it's a flashing neon sign.

The others on her flight, Jessica, Liam, Jerry, ask her how Ali is and when he's next due back. The same as everyone asks, every single day. No wonder the countdown of 'days until Ali's back' goes so painfully slowly.

Iza looks to Jessica for a bit of female camaraderie, some feeling of comfort. But she can't open her mouth to ask for it. She imagines telling Jessica what's going on. Jessica who's been there, done the long distance relationship thing and it didn't work out. Iza can't bear the thought of herself being the next in line.

It was Jessica who told Iza to keep the little things alive. The trip to Tesco and the annoying man on the till, tell Ali that, she'd say, tell him every little detail. Don't let those things die or the relationship will die as well. You have to know each other, Jessica said, inside and out. And she was right. And they did.

Ali told Iza of his housemate's antics, every night a different girl. He told her of the cleaning ladies who let themselves in to do the washing and ironing once a week; that was a surprise the first Thursday. Iza keeps Ali updated on the crew gossip, on her family gossip, anything she can think of.

What else was it Jessica had said? Be honest with each other. A nugget of wisdom for any relationship but so important when there are 5000 miles between you and the person you love. The one person you want so close and yet they are so far away.

She thinks Jessica would agree with Jack's comment: you follow a pilot where he wants to go not where you want to go, and knows it's true. They had been on the same page, wanting to live in the same area she lives in now, just maybe in a nice village on the outskirts instead. But now everything's changed and that village, that life together, is a distant memory.

Remembering all this Iza realises she can't bear to tell Jessica any of it. The flashing neon sign sits in front of her eyes again.

Iza returns home just before midnight to a text from Jack.

Dinner's ready for you, Spaghetti Bolognaise. I'm not having you tell me you ate that crew food crap. Come over when you're ready xxx

Iza reads the message and knows he'll only come over with it if she doesn't go to him so she changes quickly and heads for Jack's flat.

"I thought you needed some taking care of," he says as she steps in through the front door and he hugs her in tight.

"No Josh?"

"Not tonight, he's on earlies and wanted to get a good night sleep."

Jack leads her to his kitchen table and sits her down. He places a large plate of spaghetti bolognaise and a large glass of white wine in front of her. He then pours himself a larger glass of wine and sits down to join her.

Earlier Jack had seen Josh and hugged him a little tighter than he usually would have done. He kissed him a little longer than they usually do, just to say hello. He thought all the time what he would do if he had to choose, himself or Josh, and still couldn't decide.

"Dig in," Jack orders.

As she eats a tear escapes from Iza's eye. She thinks of how nice Jack is being when he really doesn't have to. And then her thoughts turn to Ali and another tear escapes.

"Iza? Don't cry darling."

"I can't help it. I love him," she sighs.

"I know you do sweetie, I know," Jack replies.

"I feel like if I lose him it's not just my boyfriend that I've lost. It's our life together; his family, I love his family, and our dream of a nice house, a nice car, a dog for him and a cat for me. Three kids…" Iza trails off.

"You spoke about kids?"

"Yeah." She gulps. "We had everything planned out and now he's changed his mind and it's all gone."

Jack pushes his hand across the table and strokes her arm.

"I know you love him sweetie, but I said it before, who do you love more? Him or you?" he asks as softly as possible. "You're still young, and you want to go and study and that's a great thing."

"It's just so unfair."

"Yeah."

Iza knows what Jack is trying to tell her but won't say: break up with him, for your own sake. But life and especially love is never that easy.

Jack insists she eats the rest of her pasta and then lets her go home to be alone with her thoughts. He tells her he'll be up if she wants to talk any more.

At home Iza runs a bath, surrounds herself with scented candles and pours another glass of wine. She undresses and lies down in the bath, the steaming hot water making her body tense at first and then relaxing her as the salts caress her muscles. She takes a sip of wine and feels the gentle bubbles and crisp taste in her mouth. The candles flicker around her and ooze out the sweet smell of raspberry and papaya.

She sinks her head under the water of the bath and hears the muffled sounds of the flat. She knows Ali will be asleep but she thinks of ringing him to wake him up anyway, just so she can hear his voice and not imagine it over email. She thinks better of it and gasps for breath as she comes back up and out of the water.

Again Iza finds herself sat on the edge of her bed, her laptop balancing precariously on her lap. This time her hair falls about her shoulders, wavy and wet, sticking to her bare skin; she wears an un-ironed tank top and pyjama shorts; her make-up gone, her eyes tired, dry skin showing on her forehead. She reads her message one more time.

I'm not sure what you mean about Edinburgh. I didn't realise it was set in stone? You knew Edinburgh would never be my first choice of home. I have nothing to keep me there. I don't want you to be my only friend or point of call and I've found something that I finally, truly believe I will be good at, and will enjoy. You know this job has lost its beauty for me. I would like your support in this, as I have given my support to you. I have accepted my place on the course and will be starting this

September. Will you stay down here, where we dreamt we would be together?

I love you so so much.

XXXXXXXXXXXXXXXX

She hits send.

DUB

Kate waits, tapping her newly manicured pale pink nails on the armrest of her seat at the front of the cabin. The conversation between the crew dried up half an hour ago, out of boredom. Liam flicks through a magazine abandoned on-board by a previous passenger, Jerry, to her left, lets out a loud deep sigh and the FO, Pete, new to flying and still in his own world, seems completely unaware of the tension now settling in the cabin. Kate checks her watch, again.

Ewan, the captain, puts down the company mobile phone, steps out of the cockpit and says, "Right guys, and girls, we will be ready to leave in about thirty minutes."

"Sure, there's just one small problem with that, in thirty minutes we'll go into discretion," Jerry points out to Ewan.

"Ah," he replies, wishing they'd told him sooner.

The crew have already been working for twelve hours. This is the last of a long four-sector day, and the crew are in no mood to be doing favours.

"Well I guess it's up to you then. What do you want to do? Get home, or go to a hotel?" Ewan asks.

"We're not working," Jerry states.

"What?" Ewan asks again, shocked at the abruptness.

"We're not going into our discretion, so-we're-not. We've already spoken about it as a crew and we've decided."

Pete seems to perk up at the news, Ewan takes the opposite stance. The rest of the crew watch the exchange. Liam opens his mouth and takes a breath about to say something but Pete gets there first.

"So we're night stopping?" Pete asks hopefully.

"Your first one?" Jerry asks Pete with a smile.

"Yep, awesome." Pete beams a smile back to Jerry, then notices Ewan's face and tries to remove the smile, he fails.

"It's only an hour's flight home," Ewan says.

"And we have to board the passengers and disembark them, and count the money at the end of the flight, pay it in and then check out. This is only your second flight of the day, it'll be our fourth, and to tell the truth we're all a little fecked off actually."

Ewan looks to the rest of the crew. Iza looks out of the window. Liam looks as if he's about to speak then thinks better of it and continues to read his magazine. Kate stares back at Ewan in what she hopes is a stern manner. She tries to hide her own excitement at the thought of an unscheduled night stop in Dublin.

"And you're all decided on this?" Ewan asks.

It's the captain that'll have to do all the extra paperwork tomorrow but Kate thinks that Ewan is only kicking up a fuss so he can blame the crew for the night stop, and not have the blame fall on his own head.

"Yes," Kate says.

Ewan takes a deep breath. "Ok," he says, "I'll tell ops. We might have to stay on-board until another crew arrives." Ewan returns to the cockpit.

Jerry looks over at the rest of his crew who are all now looking at him; he winks at them and then says, "Let's get ready lads."

As Kate starts to walk down the aisle to the back of the cabin Jerry grabs her arm and whispers in her ear.

"Get a couple of drinks for everyone from the bar will ya."

Kate looks back at him to make sure he's being serious, she sees his smiling face.

"Mines a G&T. Go on now," he says to her, and she makes her way to the back galley.

In the hotel Kate looks at herself in the mirror, glad that she packed a change of clothes ready for such an occasion, but is feeling sure the dress she packed was longer last time she wore it. She pulls at the hem to try and bring it down but soon gives up. Outside she has a view of the airport. She watches as the planes come and go. She wonders if one of them is the flight she was meant to be on. She takes a sip of her rum and coke, courtesy of the on-board bar. The mix of the altitude, being stuck in a metal tube with recycled air and a sudden hit of alcohol makes her head spin. She was hoping that she wasn't going to seem like a light-weight but it's too late for that now. She piles the rest of the miniatures and mixers onto a tray and carries them down the hall to Jerry's room.

Jerry's door is propped open; Kate hears the sounds of Jerry's and Pete's laughter leaking into the hallway. Kate hopes this won't be embarrassing, having spent the night with Pete the week before. So far it hasn't been much of a problem but being in close proximity like this could get awkward she thinks.

Pete hasn't changed but has just taken his epaulettes off his white shirt, now untucked, and removed his tie. He's still wearing his black pilot's trousers and shoes.

"Oh, little Katie," Jerry says, "come in."

Jerry has a whole new outfit on, new accessories and everything.

"You gotta be prepared, you never know what's going to happen," he tells Kate.

Kate notices that they both have drinks in their hands; they must've opened the mini bar. Jerry downs his drink and takes the tray from her, pouring himself another.

"I got you some beer," Kate tells Pete, "is that ok?"

"Great, yeah, thanks," he smiles at her taking one. They stand awkwardly for a moment then Pete says, "Ewan isn't going to join us. He rang me and told me he just wants an early night."

"Oh what a shame," Jerry butts in putting his arm around Kate's shoulder. "So how do you feel about Temple Bar?"

"Is that a pub or a place?" Kate asks.

"Well both actually, but basically a place with lots of pubs, in the centre of Dublin, me and ya man Pete were just talking about going there tonight if you're up for the craic?"

"We can jump straight onto the bus that stops right outside the hotel and we'll be in town in thirty minutes," Pete adds.

"Ummm, ok." Kate helps herself to another drink, excited about the night ahead but not sure how she's going to keep up with them drinking.

Iza knocks on the door and lets herself in.

"Where are your dancing shoes?" Pete asks, nodding at Iza's flip-flops, baggy trousers and top.

"I'm not feeling great. Why where are you guys going?" she replies.

"Into town. You sure you don't want to come?" Pete asks.

"No, no, I'm fine thanks. But you guys go and have fun," she says, distractedly. She heads for the balcony door and then asks, "Do you mind?"

"Not at all, actually, I'll join ya," Jerry replies, picking up his pack of cigarettes and heads outside with her. They close the door behind them and Kate and Pete are left alone in the room.

Right on cue Liam bursts into the room. "Sorry I'm late, had to call the boyf... Oh, woah, sorry am I interrupting?" he asks, laughing nervously.

"No, no," Kate almost shouts, hoping her face hasn't gone red.

"We're going into town, to Temple Bar," Pete says, taking a seat on the bed, "you coming?"

Kate decides to sit at the small table in the corner of the room and Liam joins her.

"Umm," he thinks for a minute, pouting his lips, and then replies, "ok," with a big smile.

Merrily Jerry, Pete, Liam and Kate leave Iza and Ewan at the hotel and get the bus into central Dublin.

As they walk down the main thoroughfare Jerry points out some sights.

"This here waste of time, money and space is called the 'Spire'; I've no idea what the point of it is at all." He points to the erect silver spike, shooting out of the ground in the middle of O'Connell Street.

"Here is the river Liffey, you don't want to be on your own here at night, but in the day I think it's rather lovely. Now if you keep heading that way you get to Trinity College Dublin, very fancy university, very pretty. But this is where we're going," Jerry stops his tour, and his tour party bump into each other behind him.

They gather together looking into the cobbled streets, the mass of people spilling out of doors and pubs, at the red brick buildings that now surround them.

"And here is the hotel I was telling you about. The one I woke up in as a wee young lad, next to some old naked man, god knows who he was, but it's a nice hotel, so I stole as much as I could and got the feck out of there." Jerry finishes his tour.

Jerry weaves through the crowd, leading them into a bar as packed inside as it is out. "What are you drinkin'? Guinness or Guinness?"

"Oh no, no, no," Kate says shaking her head. But Jerry carries on regardless.

"Ah go on," Jerry says.

Kate shakes her head as Jerry nods.

"I'll get ya a half," he says, "you can't come to Dublin and not have a Guinness." He winks at her again.

Kate turns to look at Liam for some back up but he just shrugs and nods to Jerry and his excited face.

"Guinness it is," Pete agrees, "I'll get the first round." And off he goes to find the bar.

The Guinness was too thick and strong for Kate, she knew it would be, so Pete helps her finish it off. He buys her a Baileys instead, not letting her spend a penny, even when she tries to insist, just like the other night. She's grateful because she doesn't really want to spend her money but she doesn't like the arm that Pete has put around her waist as he speaks to her.

The Irish cream, ordered to keep Jerry happy, has a cloudy appearance as it drifts around her glass. As she drinks it makes its way into her brain; the fog continues to swirl there.

Jerry has managed to find a guy he knows over by the bar and they chat away together, too fast, and too Irish, for the others to understand in the loud bar.

Pete's hand strokes Kate's back. As Liam speaks, Kate tries to wiggle herself free, but her small stature gets lost in the swarm of people and Pete brings her back into his arm, she can't help but smile a little.

They all talk and joke around and laugh. They have another drink, Liam's round. He buys them all doubles and a shot. They dance even though there's no dance floor and they have another drink, Kate's round. She buys them all a drink and a shot, she pretends she had her shot already at the bar but she didn't really, she had a quick glass of water, while no one was watching. They sing along to the live band that is playing, so loud that some of the other people tell them to 'shut it'. They have another drink, Jerry's round. He buys them all a drink and calls them over to the bar where they find shots, on fire, waiting for them.

Pete eyes up every attractive woman in the bar and a lot of them look back at him with smiles on their faces. Kate notices, as she did at crew night, but doesn't really mind. She's not trying to win his affection or have his attention solely on her; almost the opposite. What happened the other night, just happened, an accident almost. Kate knew Pete's reputation and that night what she wanted was just to have fun. Pete was the right guy for that night. But not tonight, or any other for that matter, the other women can have him she thinks too herself.

Liam suddenly looks at his watch in shock, it's ten past ten already. He shouts at the others to look at the time but they don't understand, their drunkenness overtaking their memory and rationality, so he pushes his wrist watch close to their faces. Jerry suddenly jumps.

"Feck."

But Kate and Pete still don't understand. They giggle at the sight of Jerry.

"We've got to go!" Jerry cries.

"Why?" Kate asks.

"We'll miss the bus!" Jerry shouts, "drink up." Jerry pushes their glasses towards their mouths, spilling Pete's Guinness down his shirt a little.

"Thank you," Liam says with a sigh of relief and quickly downs his drink.

"What are you talking about?" Pete asks.

"Last bus to the airport leaves at half ten," Jerry explains, "come on."

Jerry grabs Kate and Liam by the wrists and pushes his way through the crowd, out of the bar. The cold air hits them, sending the alcohol even further into their brain's. They trip up the street, whilst Jerry sings some Irish song Kate doesn't know. She's unsure whether it's the alcohol, the unscheduled night stop joy, or just his being Irish and back in Ireland that has brought out this new side to Jerry, but she likes it so she grabs his arm and tries to join in with the song, making up the words as she goes along. Jerry laughs at her attempts and almost misses the turning for the bus stop as he attempts to teach her the lyrics.

The bus is sitting waiting at the stop as they turn the corner.

"Quick!" shouts Liam and they all try to run towards it.

They get there just as the bus driver is about to close the door. He looks less than thrilled as the four of them stumble aboard.

The bus ride takes it out of Jerry and within ten minutes he's fallen asleep, his head resting on the window and his snoring growing steadily louder. Pete and Liam chat away. Kate can feel her head bouncing around with each turn of the bus and with every jolt in the road. She notices Pete's hand on her knee but just looks at it. As she looks up, completely lost from the conversation now, she thinks she sees Liam looking at Pete's hand and then suddenly away; she feels her face flush red. She's sure people have heard through crew night gossip about her and Pete but she's surprised how close Pete has been all night; how comfortable he's been. She looks at his face as he talks, totally engrossed in the conversation. She notices his smile and the lines that curve around the edge of his lips. His hair could use a new style she thinks but his jaw line could be that of a models. She wants to touch it, to trace it with her fingers, but she doesn't let herself.

Back in the hotel Jerry stumbles down the hallway, mumbles a good night and heads into his room. A few moments later, as Pete, Liam and Kate stand in the hallway trying to whisper, they hear Jerry's snores through the wall and they all have to suppress a laugh. Liam and Pete keep chatting like all of a sudden they're best mates. Kate tries to find an opportunity to interrupt and say good night but she can't get a word in edgeways. They don't seem to take a breath. Finally as they giggle about something she gets to talk.

"I'm going to bed guys, night night," she says with a yawn.

"Ok gorgeous, see you tomorrow," Liam replies, kissing her on the check.

Pete doesn't seem to know how to react and quickly says goodbye.

Kate starts to walk down the hallway towards her room. She watches her feet stepping one in front of the other and she can feel herself wobbling to the left, then the right, then the left again as her attempts to walk in a straight line fail miserably. All off a sudden she feels her feet lift of the ground and arms around her waist. She's being spun around and as she's put back down and able to catch her breath she realises it's Pete.

"What are you doing?" she asks.

"Coming to say good night," he replies.

"Where is Liam," she asks, trying to look past Pete down the corridor, hoping Liam isn't staring back. The hallway is empty. She looks back at Pete's face, he just stands there smiling.

She opens the door to her room on the second attempt and Pete follows her in. He closes the door and before she's even put the card in the slot for the lights Pete's mouth is on hers, kissing her and holding her body tight to his. She pushes him away.

"What are you doing?" she asks again shrugging him off and putting the lights on.

She steps into the bathroom and closes the door. She locks it. Her cosmetics are sprawled across the counter top and she remembers she hasn't got any make-up remover wipes so she just splashes her face with water and leaves her eye make-up where it is. She cleans her teeth with a travel toothbrush set and heads back into her room. Pete's lying on the bed. The curtains are closed.

"Sorry," he says, "come and talk to me." Pete pats the bed and rolls onto his back with his hands behind his head.

Kate hesitates for a moment then walks towards him.

"Close your eyes," she says.

"Why? What are you going to do to me?" he asks.

"Nothing. I'm just going to take my tights off and get under the covers," she tells him.

"Ok," Pete replies and closes his eyes with a smile.

Kate looks at him for a second, then sticks out her tongue at him to make sure he's not peaking.

"Come on," Pete says, his eyes still closed.

This makes her jump, as if he knows what she's thinking and she quickly takes of her tights and gets into bed beside him. Under the covers she can feel his weight bearing down next to her.

"Can I open my eyes yet?" he asks.

"Ok," Kate replies.

Pete opens his eyes and rolls onto his side.

"Talk to me then," he says, almost demanding her to.

"I'm too tired to talk," she says, "and too drunk".

Pete ignores this and asks, "Are you working tomorrow?"

"No. Thank god. Although they better give me a day off for flying back tomorrow."

"They will do, don't worry, they have to."

"You?" Kate asks with a yawn.

"Yeah," Pete sighs, "but this was still worth it."

"What was?" Kate asks unsure.

"The night stop. And going out in Dublin, that was fun." His voice sounds far away.

Kate feels something on her arm. It's Pete's hand. He's stroking her arm, softly, up and down.

"Stop it," she says with her eyes closed and heavy, "please."

"Stop what?"

"Stroking my arm."

"I thought you liked it?" Pete says and she can feel his warms breath on her cheek.

"Please," she repeats.

But Pete doesn't stop. He starts stroking her belly as he whispers into her ear.

"You liked it the other night. When I stroked you here… and here." His hand moves down the covers and she grabs it.

"What? He asks her. "Don't you like it?"

She doesn't know. Does she like it? He's right she did like it the other night but she wasn't lying, she's shattered, and tonight it doesn't feel the same, knowing that the rest of the crew are just a few rooms away.

Pete slides himself under the covers.

"Don't." Kate cries out, trying to move away but feeling her legs on the edge of the bed.

"It's ok," he says, "I won't look."

She tries to relax her body but she can feel his next to her. Her heads stopped making sense.

"Talk to me," she says, "just talk to me."

"What do you want to talk about?"

"Anything. Just talk to me, I want to listen."

"Ok," he says, still lying close.

Pete starts talking. Kate's not sure what about as her eyes close again and her body loosens up, sinking into the bed. She feels a light kiss on her neck, but Pete keeps talking, then another kiss on her cheek. She thinks about the night they've just had. She thought she was being quite clear that what they had was just for that one time. She'd tried to make it clear to everyone. To Jerry and Liam so they wouldn't keep looking at her funny; she felt like they were laughing at her behind her back. She thought she was making it clear to Pete as well. She wasn't flirting, she barely laughed at his jokes. She opens her eyes and Pete is leaning over her, looking into her face.

"God you're fit."

Kate puts her hands out to his chest but he's on top of her before she can push him away. Her arms feel weak. His hands reach down into her underwear.

"You like this?" he asks.

She doesn't know. She knows she doesn't want to have sex, not now, but her body is responding to his touch.

"Oh, yeah you do." Pete answers his own question.

"Stop it."

"Why?"

Kate can feel Pete moving around, pushing himself onto her through his trousers.

"Stop it," she says again.

"I know what you want," he says, his face close to hers, smiling.

He lifts himself away to pull down his clothes, and she grabs a hold of his arms.

"Hang on a minute," he says.

"No, don't," she says. Her voice cracks. "Don't," she says again. She tries to dig her nails into his arms but he mustn't feel it because he doesn't tell her it hurts.

He forces himself into her. "Don't what?" he says as he exhales.

"Don't, you know what, don't," her voice is weak.

He moves himself on top of her.

"You like this?" he asks his eyebrows raised.

She doesn't know what to do.

"Stop," she begs. "Stop."

But he doesn't stop.

She tries to kick her legs but his weight and height encompass her. She thinks about shouting, screaming, but she doesn't want anyone to find her like this.

"No." She tries to grab his hips.

He groans.

"Don't." She tries to lean up on her elbows.

He pushes her back down.

"Stop!" She pulls her face away from his, into the pillow.

He sighs and his body falls on top of hers.

After a moment he rolls off and lies next to her.

"Talk to me," he says.

She's not sure if she's even capable of talking anymore but some words do escape her.

"I'm tired."

"Ok." He replies.

He sits up on the bed, pulling his trousers back up as he does, and watches her. She turns her face away from him but doesn't close her eyes.

Pete stands up and without looking back leaves the room. Closing the door behind him.

Kate waits a moment and then gets out of bed, she checks the door is properly closed, and puts the safety latch on it as well.

As she gets back into bed she turns off the light. Exhausted, her eyes close and she falls asleep.

The hotel room phone rings waking Kate up with a start. She picks it up.

"This is your wake up call," the receptionist says.

Confused Kate looks at the time, half seven, and starts to reply.

"Thank you," but before she's finished the receptionist hangs up the phone.

She rubs her eyes which leave a black smudge on her fingers.

"Shit." She says to herself then the thought of Pete jumps into her head.

She sits up straight, quick, in her bed. He's not there. She breaths out, unaware she'd been holding her breath. She gets up, and as she stands her head throbs. Should've expected that she thinks and she walks to the bathroom.

In the mirror she looks back at herself, messy hair, make up down her face and her insides shoot downwards as she remembers last night. She shuts her eyes hard and tells herself not to think about it. Don't.

She re-applies her make-up, puts her hair into a bun, pulls on yesterday's tights, shirt, and uniform and calls Jerry.

"Urgh." Comes his reply down the other end of the phone.

"Sorry, did I wake you?" she asks.

"No, I'm awake. I'm not sure if I'm actually alive though," he replies.

Kate laughs, and her insides start to feel a touch lighter.

"You coming down for breakfast?" she asks him.

"Probably should, yeah. Meet you down there in ten minutes or so?"

"Ok," she says, and as she hangs up the phone she hears him on the other end, his voice getting farther and farther away.

"Bye, bye, bye, bye, bye, bye, bye."

Kate packs up her suitcase, her make-up and last night's clothes, swallows two painkillers, and makes her way down to the hotel dining hall, with butterflies in her stomach. She spots Liam first, standing beside the cooked breakfast.

"Best part about night stops," Liam says, "the fried breakfast."

He piles his plate up high with food, Kate looks at it, not sure she'll be able to stomach anything.

"How you feeling this morning?" he asks.

"Terrible," she replies, "I'm never drinking Guinness again!"

Liam laughs. He leads her over to his table and Kate finds Iza sat there already with a cup of coffee.

"Hey," Iza says with a smile.

Kate thinks she looks slightly happier than yesterday but no less tired.

"Hey. Did you manage to have a nice quite night?" Kate asks.

"Yes thank you. I ended up watching *Father Ted*, how ironic right?" Iza replies.

"No you didn't, feck off." Jerry appears behind Kate. "Hi gorgeous," he says, giving Kate a kiss. He leans over to Iza and kisses her cheek too.

"How are you all feeling today then?" Iza asks.

Kate and Jerry let out a groan. Only Liam actually replies with words.

"Fine, actually," he says with a mouthful off scrambled eggs. "Oh hey," he says.

"Hi," Ewan replies, making Kate jump.

As she turns around she sees Pete standing next to him. They're both in there pilots' uniforms, and the few other people in the restaurant look around at them.

"Hi," says Pete. He waves at everyone around the table then hugs Kate. She stiffens up and catches Jerry's eye. He smiles at her.

As Pete lets go, Kate realises Ewan is watching, she looks away.

"Anyone else want some coffee?" Iza asks.

Kate could kiss her for breaking the tension, or is it just her that can feel it? She doesn't know.

"Can I talk to you for a moment?" Kate directs her question towards Iza who replies with a nod and follows Kate into the hallway.

Kate looks at Iza and prepares to tell her about last night, about Pete. A moment ago she was positive Iza would believe her and tell her its ok, maybe she'd give her a hug and tell her what to do next. But what should she do next, what could she do? And what will Iza even think when she tells her? Doubts flood into Kate's brain, all the messages she'd been trying not to think about throughout breakfast flash before her. Why didn't you stop him? Why didn't you scream louder? Why did you let this happen to yourself?

"Kate?" Iza asks.

Kate's sudden rush of warmth towards Iza and the hope that everything will be ok falls away. She knows why she didn't scream louder, and why her words feel like glue within her mouth. Because no one will believe her.

"Do you have a sanitary towel?" the words burst out of Kate's mouth. "I didn't plan ahead for the night stop, so I don't have enough," Kate lies.

"Oh sure," Iza fumbles in her handbag, "Here you go."

Kate takes the sanitary towel and quickly pushes it into her own handbag. Wishing she could just say it out loud. But she can't.

"Was that all?" Iza asks, holding eye contact.

"Yeah, thanks."

When everyone has finished their breakfasts they bring their bags down from their rooms, ready to

111

check out, get on the shuttle bus and get themselves home.

On board, Kate can feel the tears waiting to escape and it takes all her energy to not let them spill out. She smiles a cabin crew smile, plastering it across her face and welcomes the passengers on board.

FAO

Josh watches Suzi as she chats away, re-stocking the carts and preparing them for the second food service. In the cabin Charlie and Gabriella have just started the duty free service and seem to be doing well. Suzi hasn't mentioned anything about Charlie or the rumours, not yet, though Josh knows she knows. Jack told him. He does notice, however, her quick glances in Charlie's direction, her look of contempt, the way her upper lip curls. Josh pretends to listen, but knows he's not needed for this conversation. None of Suzi's absent-minded chatter touches on what's really going on at the moment. He knows about the kiss that happened between her and that new captain, Mason. Jack told him that too. He wonders why she hasn't told him herself. She has nothing to be ashamed of.

He notices then how young Suzi really is; and how old he feels in comparison, though there's only five years difference between them. It's naive of her not to confront Charlie, to let the rumours spread like this, he thinks. People are saying horrible things: that she asked for it, that she's a slag. He does, however, understand why she keeps her mouth shut. The same reason he keeps his mouth shut, even when he knows others are taking him for a ride. Because, the fear is, if you open your mouth you risk losing everything – both bad and good.

Josh senses that his eyes have glazed over, and when he blinks and brings himself back to the present he notices that he's been staring at a women's breasts in the front row. She is staring back at him angrily. I'm gay, you twat, he thinks to himself, but instead of shouting out as he would like to do, he gives her a quick apologetic smile and turns away.

A call bell chimes and without thinking Josh and Suzi both look up and check where it is. Charlie has got there first. Josh and Suzi look away, continuing their one sided conversation. Then someone screams.

Josh and Suzi whirl around again and the hairs on the back of their necks shoot up, sending shivers through their bodies. Another passenger screams further down the plane; people look around, confused. Josh sees a male passenger pull at Charlie and feels his jaw clench. What is going on?

The man points out of the window and almost simultaneously Charlie straightens up, her eyes wide and she marches up to the front of the cabin. Passengers try to get out of their seats in front of her, in her way, calling out to her. "What's happening?" They paw at her uniform.

She pushes past them, saying, "Remain in your seats. Everything's under control." She lies.

Josh, seeing Charlie's white face approach him grabs a hold of her arms. "What's wrong?"

Quietly, so as not to spread the panic, she says to Josh, "The right hand side engine is on fire. You need to call the Captain." Her voice trails off into a whimper.

Josh stares at her for a moment then nods sharply. He turns around and dials the flight deck on the PA phone but there's no reply; biting his lip he hangs on.

Suzi watches Charlie, still with a look of disgust upon her face. She knows, Suzi thinks, she knows I know. But now is not the time.

"Put the trolleys away," Charlie says.

For a second Suzi hesitates, not wanting to take orders from Charlie, but begrudgingly she obeys, working fast.

"I'm going down the back," Charlie tells Josh who is still waiting, still biting his lip so hard it's almost bleeding.

"Wait," he says, trying to reach out to her, "what did you actually see?"

"Flames," Charlie replies, trying to keep her voice low without it breaking, "coming out of the engine. And some smoke."

He nods at her and she makes her way back down the cabin to Gabriella to tell her to put the duty free-carts away as well.

Suzi looks down the aisle and sees passengers holding onto their arm rests so tightly their knuckles are turning white, matching their colourless faces. Some call out to her as she tries to keep a smile on her face. The sounds usually reserved for small children and babies appear on the lips of the adults aboard: crying, spluttering, whimpering.

Suzi takes a deep breath and gives herself a pep talk: you chose this job, you trained for this, now go out and deal with it. The anger she feels for Charlie is fuelling her, pushing her to be better than Charlie. She fixes a smile to her face, pulls her jacket on and leaves the galley to answer call bells and questions.

Josh is still trying to reach the flight deck. He looks at his watch, it seems to have slowed down. It's almost stopped ticking but the battery is brand new. Pick up the phone for fuck sake, Josh begs the pilots to answer. No news is good news, he tells himself. They are probably talking to Air Traffic Control and trying to sort it out, and pressing a fuck load of buttons. Unless they're unconscious and that's why they're not picking up. Fuck, fuck, fuck, he panics.

Josh looks down the aisle and sees both Charlie and Gabriella in the back galley looking up at him, watching, waiting.

A voice sounds on the other end of the phone, Ashleah's, the first officer, "Josh, we know, we're dealing with it. What can you see?"

She sounds so calm, so efficient, he thinks. In the background he can hear chiming from the on board systems.

"Charlie, and some passengers, saw flames and smoke coming from the inside of the engine.

116

That's all I know," he replies, trying hard not to let his voice shake.

"Ok. Great thanks. We'll call you back," Ashleah says and hangs up.

Josh takes a breath; he hears the worried voices of the passengers rising. He calls the back galley. "Ashleah says they're dealing with it and will call me back. One of you stay in the back galley, the other help Suzi keep people calm, move them if necessary. Put your jackets on and get your high-vis ready." Josh speaks in short, sharp, commands. He goes to put the phone down then asks, "Are you ok?"

Charlie looks at Gabriella.

"We're fine. Are you ok?" Charlie replies trying to stay confident in herself, if for no one else's sake then for Josh. She knows she has more experience than Suzi and Gabriella put together and now is the time to use it.

"I'm fine." The adrenaline in Josh rises and a hit of confidence flows through him.

Suzi and Charlie make their way through the plane, call bells chime all around them as people screech and sob. They repeat their mantras over and over again to the passengers as calmly as they can manage. "Everything's under control. The pilots are aware and are dealing with the situation. Would you like to change seats? Please leave your baggage where it is.

We're trained to deal with situations like this so please just stay as you are."

Charlie helps a woman and her small child change seats and knocks into Suzi as she does this, sending Suzi off balance. Suzi straightens up, forgetting herself for a moment, her face feeling hot, she stares straight into Charlie's eyes.

"I'm sorry," Charlie says, trying to take hold of Suzi's arm but Suzi pulls away.

Suzi knows now is not the time. She knows the passengers must be watching, already scared and now even more confused. She knows that she is in uniform and has a job to do and so she pulls herself up tall. Still holding Charlie's gaze she promises to herself to get a real apology, when this is over. When they and everyone around them are safe, but for now, for now, sorry will do.

Josh's voice sounds out across the cabin.

"Ladies and Gentlemen. We are aware there is a situation on board. We are working very hard to alleviate this. Please listen to the instructions of your cabin crew and remain in your seats." Josh wonders if that was the right thing to do. They don't teach you this part in training; the waiting is so much longer than you can imagine and the intense desire to go and gawk for yourself at the fire, and scream at the sight of it, like the passengers is overwhelming.

Josh looks around his galley, anything to not look at his watch, and wait for *that* call. He clears his and Suzi's tea cups away and her make-up bag which she had out on the side. He makes sure all the clips are down, that everything is secure, that all brakes on the carts are on. He puts his jacket on and looks down the cabin.

Gabriella watches him from the back galley; their eyes meet. Josh attempts a smile but he's not sure if it works. He feels his chest, heavy, rise and fall.

"Excuse me young man," an elderly lady in the front row asks him, "but what's going on?"

"We have a slight situation on board. I'm waiting to hear from our Captain and when I do I can let everyone know." If she doesn't know about the fire, don't panic her just yet he tells himself.

"Are you sure you're ok?" she asks.

"I'm fine, thank you."

"You're shaking."

Josh realises she's right. He smiles at her but quickly steps away. He looks at his watch, only five minutes have passed, it feels like at least half an hour.

Suddenly the Captain's voice is heard over the PA. "Number One to the cockpit immediately."

Josh, clenching his fists, trying to stop the shaking, almost jumps out of his skin. He composes himself, smiles at the lady in the front row and enters the cockpit.

The passengers' cries die down but the tension in their faces grows. Sobs fade away into shock and an eerie stillness comes over the cabin.

Charlie restrains herself from holding Gabriella's hand or hugging her tight and not letting go. She wishes that she could be in the cockpit instead of Jack right now. She wishes she could be close to Ian, so he could look into her eyes and tell her that everything is going to be ok, that they are all going to be ok, but mostly that they, she and Ian, are going to be ok. She wishes she could believe her fantasies.

As Josh exits the cockpit he finds Suzi, Charlie and Gabriella all in the front galley awaiting his instructions.

"Ok. I'm going to give you the same briefing Ashleah has just given me." He looks at his crew and for a split second feels relief. He knows he can trust them to do as he says, he knows they are all competent at their jobs. This could be a lot worse.

"The nature is: the engine on the right hand side has caught fire, Ian has turned this engine off. The intentions are: We are going to prepare for a pre-planned emergency landing; we are diverting to Bilbao in Spain. The time available is: eighteen minutes to landing. No special instructions at this time. So please set your watches to my time; which is set to Ian's time."

The crew all bunch in together to check the time on their watches against each other's. Suzi makes sure not to let Charlie's arm touch her own.

"Any questions?" Josh asks.

"Are we going to evacuate?" Gabriella asks.

"I don't know but be prepared. And be prepared to block the exits on the right hand side."

All three nod and Josh asks them to repeat his instructions back to him.

"If you haven't done already, secure your galley," he says to Gabriella and Charlie. "We all need to get our high-vis jackets on and when you're ready make your way into the cabin."

Josh, now with instructions and some reassurance from Ian and Ashleah feels his training kick in, he takes command, he's in control. He sneaks a look down at his hands, steady as a rock and feels his breathing return to normal.

The cabin crew place themselves in position for their safety demo, this time ready to brief the passengers for their emergency landing. Every pair of eyes is now on them. No one is reading, texting or talking as many were during their initial demo. The passengers watch in horror and awe.

"Ladies and Gentlemen, listen very carefully and follow my instructions." Josh asserts himself over the PA. "The captain has informed me that will we be making an emergency landing into Bilbao Airport in sixteen minutes time." The passengers' cries start up again, blubbering and bawling.

"Please, listen very carefully and follow my instructions." Josh repeats himself, louder this time as he starts the demo.

"Fasten your seat belt. Ensure your chair is in the upright position with the arm rest down and the tray table folded away. The window blind must be fully open. All electronic equipment must be turned off now. Please remove head phones from your ears. Ensure all carry-on items are placed well under the seat in front of you."

The crew start pushing chairs into the up-right position, forcing baggage under the seats in front, checking seat belts. Suzi realises her hands are clenching just a little too tightly and her arms are ridged with the pressure. She tries to stretch them out and feels the blood pulsing through to her fingertips.

Josh pauses until his crew are back in their places. In training he was always nervous about making this announcement, and that was just in front of his fellow cabin crew. He was always scared he'd get something wrong, forgetting the most important thing. But standing up in front of his crew and passengers now it all makes sense. Breathe. When he had spoken to Ashleah, face to face, she had seemed calm, methodical even. Josh told himself to soak it up and stay that way. Keep your voice calm, he tells himself now, and the passengers will stay calm.

"There are eight emergency exits on board this air craft. Two at the front of the cabin, two at the back of the cabin and four over wing window exits." The crew point these out, as they did at the beginning of the flight. "Exit signs and low level lighting will guide you to these exits."

"We are now going to show you the brace position which is the best position for landing. The crew will demonstrate the position and then I will repeat the instructions so that you can practise."

Suzi, Charlie and Gabriella feel the eyes of each passenger burning into them; faces engrained on their brains to forever remind them of this moment. Their smiles are gone.

Charlie wonders what Ian is doing now, if he's thinking of her. If he wishes he could run out into the cabin just to make sure she's ok. She knows he's busy, more than busy, but she hopes that she is there, somewhere in his thoughts.

"Fasten your seat belt." The cabin crew mime this. "Place your feet flat on the floor. Bend forward until your head touches the chair in front of you or your chest touches your knees. Place one hand on top of the other on top of your head. DO NOT interlock your fingers. Pull your elbows in tightly."

The cabin crew stand in front of the passengers with their arms curled over their heads until Josh finishes his instructions. Charlie hesitates a moment, fighting back a tear, then releases her arms ready to get the passengers into the brace position.

Suzi, beyond tears, now feels numb. All she can think of is the next step of the demo, the next bit of training, and she keeps going.

Josh repeats the instructions and the crew push and pull the passengers into the correct position, no time for stubbornness or incorrect placement. Josh waits, watching. His heart beating fast. Do as you are told, he thinks, this could save your life.

"Now, sit back up and look at me. You will be given the command to brace one minute before landing. Remain in this position until the aircraft has come to a complete stop. Remain in your seats, and await further instructions."

"If the captain gives the command to evacuate, open your seat belt, leave everything behind, go to the nearest exit, get out and move as far away from the aircraft as possible." Josh wants to repeat himself as he knows they will not listen to this, bags will be flying everywhere, people will be pushing and screaming but all he can do, in the end, is rely on his crew to get them out as quickly as possible.

"Please listen to your cabin crew and comply with anything they say. They have been trained to deal with this situation."

Charlie takes a deep breath and tries to smile. I have been trained to deal with this, she thinks, but I never, ever, thought it would happen, not to me.

"Cabin crew ABP brief." Josh finishes his announcement and asks his crew to select able-bodied persons to assist them in opening their doors if necessary. He has to do the same.

He checks his watch, eleven minutes to landing.

He picks out four strong men, not looking at their muscles for fun but necessity now; they need to help in getting the door open. He looks at the elderly couple in the front row; they have to move.

He asks one of the men he has picked out, "I may need assistance in getting the door open when we are on the ground. Would you be willing to help me?"

"No." The man replies, quickly, simply.

Great it's going to be like that. He turns to his next candidate. It's a yes and the next is a yes too. His forth says no again but behind him two more men volunteer. Thank god. He has his ABPs.

Ten minutes to landing.

He brings the men to the front galley and moves the elderly couple into two of their seats. They now have front row seats in case he needs them. Luckily this flight isn't packed with happy holiday families.

Each cabin crew member briefs their ABP's on when to open the door: if the captain calls to evacuate and the crew are unable to open the door.

How to open the door: hold onto the handle on the aircraft and with the other hand pull the red handle up. If the door doesn't instantly open, push it with one hand, help each other. And what to expect: the slide should inflate; if it's doesn't, pull the red handle on the floor. Cross your arms and step out of the aircraft on to the slide, get as far away as possible and tell others to follow you. If you can't use the exit tell people to use another one. Please take me with you.

All of the ABP's look perplexed. But with a focus in mind they concentrate on the task in hand rather than panicking about the impending situation. They repeat their instructions back to the crew, helping each other out. Once more they are asked are they willing to help? Yes. And are then asked to return to their seats.

Six minutes to landing.

Suzi, Charlie and Gabriella make their way through the cabin: helping mums with their babies and their modified brace positions; checking that the cabin is secure; seats, tables and blinds are in the right position; bags are put away; reassuring those who are crying, whilst trying not to cry themselves.

As she makes her way through the cabin, Charlie can't help but sneak a look out the window where she first saw the fire. Loudly she breathes a sigh of relief, yes there is smoke but unless she's mistaken there are no more flames. Turning the engine off must have helped she thinks. I'm going to be ok, we're all going to be ok. She lets a small smile slip from her lips and knows that when she lands safely, she won't care who knows, or who sees, she's going to run into Ian's arms and kiss him and not let go; because she needs him and she has to believe he needs her too.

Suzi talks to a woman who is hyperventilating, trying to get her to talk back and to concentrate on that rather than her breathing. It slows down just as Josh calls over the PA, "cabin crew landing positions."

She knows she must take her seat but looking into the woman's panic-stricken face she wishes she could stay. She asks another passenger to hold the woman's hand and gets them to breathe slowly and count their breaths up to ten and repeat. As she watches the passengers, strangers, comfort each other, she takes a small breath and feels her shoulders relax, the tension that has been building within her escapes a little.

As Suzi reaches the front galley she takes her seat next to Josh. They look at each other and grab each other's hand, just for a second, giving a quick squeeze, then they place their hands under their legs and into their own brace position.

In a moment of calm Josh lets his thoughts drift onto Jack and he closes his eyes. Wishing he'd said 'I love you' more, wishing he'd gone out with Jack more, doing things Jack wanted to do, instead of being lazy and staying in every night. He tells himself he can change and when he lands and gets home, things will change. Maybe Jack will stop the affairs and they can be like they used to be. He holds Jack in his mind and for the first time has the urge to tell someone. To get it out.

"I know," Josh says to Suzi opening his eyes. Her concentrated face is suddenly perplexed.

"I know," he repeats, "about Jack and Ben."

Suzi, not knowing what to say, says nothing.

"I thought you knew, its ok." He adds, as she starts to try and explain, then stops herself again.

"I just wanted someone to know, just in case. I still love him though, and I want him to be happy, that's why I can't just let him go," Josh says.

He checks his watch, ten seconds till they start shouting.

"He loves you too," Suzi says finally.

One minute till landing.

"Brace, brace. Brace, brace. Brace, brace. Brace, brace. Brace, brace. Brace, brace." Gabriella and Charlie's shouts from the back galley are matched by Josh and Suzi's from the front.

"Brace, brace. Brace, brace. Brace, brace. Brace, brace. Brace, brace. Brace, brace."

Their mouths become dry, hoarse, but they continue to shout. Out the corner of their eyes, through the small windows in the aircraft doors, they see the ground getting closer. They know that all airport traffic will have been suspended and that on the ground, sirens blaring, fire trucks will be racing the aircraft as it comes in over their heads.

In the cockpit, the radio altimeter counts down the distance in feet from the ground; fifty, forty, thirty, twenty, ten.

The aircraft touches the runway and lands. The crew continue to shout: "Brace, brace. Brace, brace. Brace, brace. Brace, brace. Brace, brace. Brace, brace."

They are praying in their heads that the plane will stop.

It does, and for a moment all is silent.

Acknowledgements

First off I would like to thank Tom Harbour. My Tom Tom. You showed me the true meaning of friendship: always being there for me with a shoulder to cry on; always ready to put another drink in my hand and lead me onto the dance floor. I couldn't have got through my short lived flying career without you by my side. From the bottom of my heart, thank you.

Thank you to Zuzana Sucha for taking me to my first crew night and many more after that. For letting me stay in your spare bedroom so many times it was renamed 'Emma's room'. Thank you for helping me make sense of a lot of things and always knowing how to cheer me up in my darkest moments.

Thank you to Kerry Hughes for taking me in and becoming a big sister to me. For always providing wise words; for always being able to make me laugh so much my cheeks hurt; and for standing up for me, adamantly, until the very end.

Thank you to Matt Malley for your advice and help when writing this book, for never judging me and for always having a cupboard (or two) full of alcohol at the ready.

I would like to thank my parents who have never doubted me; always stood by my side whatever crazy decisions I made; for believing me, unconditionally; and for pushing me to be the best I can be. I am eternally grateful and know how incredibly lucky I am to have you as parents. I would not be who I am today without you, and I don't just mean genetically.

I would also like to thank my boyfriend Kris Doe. He has had to put up with the aftermath of my 'flying career'; the loss and heartbreak, the repeated telling of stories that start 'when I was cabin crew…' and the rebuilding of myself anew. He has supported me constantly and never shies away when I share my deepest darkest thoughts, he only holds me closer. I am forever grateful at how much you have given me. We've got super love (because love isn't a big enough word).

Finally I would like to thank Vicky Grut who mentored me, provided constructive criticism - which was always right - and helped edit this book even after I had finished my degree when she really didn't have to reply to my emails. She worked so hard, and pushed me to really create something I am so proud of. She gave me the wonderful gift of self-belief by believing in me and this book.

For news on Living the Dream or Emma Franieczek follow

@esfranieczek on twitter

Or

Facebook.com/LivingtheDreamBook

24105537R00087

Printed in Poland
by Amazon Fulfillment
Poland Sp. z o.o., Wrocław